BEWITCHED

The handsome Marquis of Ruckley was in a fit of temper.
He raced his horses up the drive to his country estate
with such speed he couldn't swerve to avoid the girl in
the path of his carriage.

Greatly relieved she was still alive, the Marquis carried
the beautiful girl up to one of his guest bedrooms. When
she recovered consciousness the next morning, Ruckley
discovered that his emergency houseguest was a gypsy.

His unfortunate accident could turn out to be a stroke of
luck: only the day before at his London club, the Marquis
had bet he could pass off a common girl as a lady of
quality.

The enchanting, intelligent gypsy was perfect for the
impersonation. What an easy way to win a thousand
pounds! But the Marquis hadn't wagered on falling madly
in love with his pretty imposter.

BARBARA CARTLAND

Bantam Books by Barbara Cartland
Ask your bookseller for the books you have missed

Bewitched
Barbara Cartland

BEWITCHED
A Bantam Book / March 1975

Published simultaneously in the United States and Canada

Bantam Books are published by Bantam Books, Inc. Its trade-
mark, consisting of the words "Bantam Books" and the por-
trayal of a bantam, is registered in the United States Patent
Office and in other countries. Marca Registrada. Bantam
Books, Inc., 666 Fifth Avenue, New York, New York 10019.

PRINTED IN THE UNITED STATES OF AMERICA

Author's Note

I am indebted for the facts about the Gypsies, especially about the Kalderash and those in Russia, to the works of Jean-Paul Clebert, C.G. Leyland, John Hoyland and George Borrow.

I know myself how strictly the true Romanys keep to their Moral Code. In 1960 I fought a bitter, lengthy battle for Gypsy Camps so that their children could be educated. I considered it a gross injustice that any race of people should be moved every twenty-four hours or pay exorbitant fines. I was opposed and abused over my championship for three years.

In 1964 I founded the first Gypsy Romany Camp in the world near Hatfield in Hertfordshire, which the Gypsies themselves christened 'Barbaraville.' I was helped by the Earl of Birkenhead and the Earl of Onslow. Entirely due to our efforts the Minister of Housing and Local Government issued a Directive—which then became Law—that all County Councils must provide camps for their local Gypsies. Hertfordshire now has five camps and other Counties are following suit.

The Betting-Book at White's Club still exists. The Bets recorded in this novel, other than the one referring to the plot, are genuine.

Chapter One
1818

"I must say, Fabius," Captain Charles Collington remarked, "this is the best Port you have ever offered me."

"I am glad you appreciate it," the Marquis of Ruckley replied.

With the candles from two silver candelabra on the polished table lighting his face, it was impossible to imagine any Gentleman of Fashion could be more handsome or more elegant.

His high cravat was tied in the intricate manner which was the envy of the younger Dandies, the points of his collar high against the sharp line of his firm, almost aggressive chin.

"My father was wise enough," the Marquis went on, "to put down a pipe of this particular wine, and in my opinion it is now worth drinking."

Captain Charles Collington laughed.

"At one time," he said, "we would have been prepared to think any wine delectable after that unspeakable rubbish we drank with the Army in Portugal."

"We were glad enough to find a bottle of anything," the Marquis replied dryly. "I was always convinced that the peasants hid their stores from us."

"Of course they did," Charles Collington agreed. "Would you not have done the same if an Army of foreigners was drinking your country dry?"

"I remembered in the summer when we were down on those dusty plains," the Marquis remarked reminiscently, "feeling so damned thirsty that the mere thought of Prinny swilling champagne at Carlton House used to make me grind my teeth with rage."

"A great many thoughts about 'Gentlemen in England now a-bed,' made me do the same," his friend replied.

The Marquis poured himself out another glass of Port and passed the cut-glass decanter.

"All the same, Charles, I often regret we are not still at war."

"Good God, what an assertion!" Charles Collington exclaimed. "After eight years in the Army I do not mind telling you that I have had enough of it!"

"Going to buy yourself out?" the Marquis asked.

"I might," Captain Collington replied cautiously, "but at the same time I have not enough money to do nothing."

"You mean that you might spend what you do possess drinking and gambling?" the Marquis questioned. "There is nothing more expensive than leisure."

"That is just what I have been thinking," Charles Collington agreed.

"I have been thinking about it too," the Marquis went on, "not because I cannot afford to do nothing, but because it is so damned boring!"

"Really, Fabius, that is doing it a bit brown!" his friend protested. "You have large estates, some first-class racehorses, you are the pride of the Four-in-Hand Club and acknowledged to be the best game-shot in England. What more do you want?"

There was a silence and then the Marquis said:

"I am not certain, but I do know it is not enough!"

"Are you hipped in love?" Captain Collington asked cautiously.

"Good God, no!" the Marquis exclaimed. "What you call 'love' is the least of my troubles."

"I thought it seemed unlikely," his friend said with

2

a laugh. "You are too good-looking! That is what is wrong with you, Fabius. You have only to smile at a woman and she is ready to cast herself into your arms or march you up the aisle!"

The Marquis did not reply.

There was a frown between his eyes as he stared reflectively at his glass of Port.

Since he was one of the greatest matrimonial catches in the *Beau Monde*, it was not surprising that a large number of females were, as Captain Collington had put it, ready to throw themselves into his arms if he so much as looked in their direction.

The Marquis, however, was known to be extremely fastidious.

He had, since the war had ended, spent much of his time in London and had therefore become involved in a number of amatory adventures. These had naturally been gossiped about in the smart Social circle in which he moved.

But there had been no open scandal because either the Marquis had been exceptionally discreet, or the ladies in question had complaisant husbands.

As was the fashion, the Marquis kept a mistress in a house he provided for her, and in the more exclusive night resorts he was a familiar figure.

But at the same time there was always something reserved, or perhaps the right word was "aloof," about him which made women of every class feel in some extraordinary way that they were not good enough for him.

Among the members of the Corps de Ballet, who were so attractive that they were courted by all the Beaux and Dandies of St. James's, the Marquis was known, behind his back, as "Lord High and Mighty."

It was perhaps significant that none of his friends had been brave enough to inform him that this was his nick-name.

Looking across the table at him now, Captain Collington thought it was true that the Marquis had, while he was in the Army, appeared to be much happier and more carefree than he was at the moment.

"You know what is wrong with you, Fabius?" he said suddenly. "You ought to get married!"

"Get married?" the Marquis exclaimed, obviously startled at the idea.

"You are twenty-seven," Captain Collington said. "We are the same age and we are both in fact getting on in years. A whole generation of beardless boys has come after us. They are snapping up the heiresses and considering themselves arbiters of fashion."

"Most of them would run a mile if they heard a shot fired in anger," the Marquis said scathingly.

"That is not entirely true," Captain Collington protested. "At the same time I must admit that most of them seem a trifle immature. There is no doubt, Fabius, that war ages a man."

The Marquis smiled. It gave him a kind of raffish, beguiling quality which his face did not have in repose.

"So you think marriage is the cure for all our ills?"

"I did not say that," Charles Collington said. "I merely suggested it as an alternative to your boredom."

The Marquis threw back his head and laughed.

"I think the remedy would be far worse than the disease! Can you imagine what it would be like to be tied to one woman indefinitely?"

"All the same, Fabius, you will have to produce an heir."

The Marquis was suddenly serious.

"You are thinking of Jethro?"

"I am!" Charles Collington replied. "I suppose you know he was borrowing heavily on the chance that you would be killed before the end of the war?"

"I am aware of that," the Marquis said. "If there was one thing which made me determined that Napoleon's troops should not blow a hole through me,

4

it was the thought of Jethro setting himself up at Ruckley as the Sixth Marquis."

"I agree, the idea is quite intolerable."

Charles Collington finished his glass of Port before adding:

"We cannot sit here all night glooming over your unpleasant cousin, or wondering how to solve the problem of your ennui. How shall we amuse ourselves?"

The Marquis glanced at the clock on the mantelshelf.

"I thought we might go to the Opera House when the performance is ended. There is a rather attractive red-head I contemplated taking out to supper."

"I know the one you mean," Charles Collington said. "She comes from Vienna and she should certainly sweep away your doldrums for tonight at least!"

"She may do that later," the Marquis said. "It is the boredom of talking to those pretty doves, especially the foreign ones, which makes the hours pass slowly. You had best join me at supper, Charles. Is there not someone in the Company who takes your fancy?"

"I seem to have exhausted most of the attractive ones already," Charles Collington said. "I agree with you, Fabius, one really has nothing to say to them."

The Marquis sighed.

" 'You think I pretty—yes?' " he mimicked with a broken accent. " 'You give me nice brooch? So very hard for me pay ze rent!' Oh, God, I have listened to the whole gamut of it!"

"I expect they think you are a soft-touch!" Charles Collington laughed. "At the same time it is always amusing to speculate if they will be more entertaining than the Fashionable Impure with whom one spent the previous night, or the bit o'muslin one entertained the night before that."

"You know the trouble with you, Charles," the Marquis remarked, "is that you are becoming a regular Casanova! You tell me I ought to settle down! What

5

about you? You are quite warm enough in the pocket, or at any rate you will be when your father dies."

"He is extremely hale and hearty at sixty-five," Charles Collington replied, "and I have no intention of saddling myself with the expense of a wife and family until I can afford them. It is another kettle of fish where you are concerned."

"It is not a question of affording them, it is enduring them," the Marquis said. "A very different thing, Charles."

He pushed back his chair and stood up.

"Come on then, let us hope that this evening will sweep away the dismal idea that we are getting too old to enjoy the fluffy frivolities of the Corps de Ballet."

"The trouble with you," Charles Collington said as he rose from the table, "is that you do not drink enough!"

"I know," the Marquis answered, "and perhaps that is another pointer to the fact that I am getting old. I dislike waking up in the morning with a splitting head."

"We are two decrepit old campaigners from a war that most people are trying to forget," Charles Collington said solemnly. "Before we go to the Opera House, let us look in at White's and see if there are any other veterans of Wellington's Army feeling as we do."

"That is not a bad idea," the Marquis agreed.

In the Hall of the Marquis's house in Berkeley Square, there were a Butler and four footmen in attendance.

One handed the Marquis his high-crowned hat, and he refused the suggestion of a cape to wear over his long-tailed close-fitting evening coat.

Setting his hat firmly on his dark head, the Marquis walked ahead of Captain Collington.

Outside in Berkeley Square a carriage was waiting, and as he appeared a footman hurried to open the door.

A red carpet had been run across the pavement, but as the Marquis stepped onto it he suddenly remembered that he had not told the Butler that he wished to be called particularly early next morning.

He proposed to attend a Mill that was being held at Wimbledon Common and it necessitated his leaving London by eight-thirty at the latest.

He turned back.

"I wish to be awakened at seven . . ." he began.

As he spoke there was a resounding crash behind him.

A large piece of masonry had fallen from the upper part of the house with a deafening noise and in a cloud of dust onto the very spot where he had stood a second earlier.

Splinters from the stone spatted his legs, and there was dust on his immaculate evening clothes.

"What the devil was that?" Charles Collington ejaculated.

The footmen had all jumped and the Butler with a note of deep concern in his voice asked:

"You're not hurt, M'Lord?"

"No indeed," the Marquis replied calmly. "Although if I had not turned back to speak to you, Burton, I might easily have received the full force of that coping stone, or whatever it was."

"Indeed, Your Lordship's had an extremely fortunate escape!"

"It must have been loose and perhaps the wind blew it from the top of the house," Charles Collington suggested.

"I cannot understand it, Sir," the Butler replied. "On his Lordship's orders the roof was overhauled only a month ago. Surely if there had been anything amiss the workmen would have reported the matter?"

"They should indeed," the Marquis said.

He looked down at the heavy stone as it lay broken but ominously menacing on the red carpet.

The noise had frightened the horses and the coach-

7

man was having trouble getting them under control again.

The footman who had been about to open the door was looking at the scene with a dazed expression on his face.

Charles Collington walked forward to stand beside the Marquis.

"If that had hit you, Fabius, it would undoubtedly have killed you."

"That is just what I was thinking," the Marquis said.

He stood patiently while a flunkey brushed the dust from his clothes; then he stepped over the debris and went towards the carriage.

He settled himself comfortably inside, putting his feet up on the opposite seat.

"You had a lucky escape, Fabius," Charles Collington said as they drove off.

The Marquis did not answer. He appeared to be deep in thought.

The carriage, a D'Orsay Cabriolet which was the latest fashion amongst the aristocracy, was extremely comfortable and built for speed.

The two horses drawing it were examples of the outstanding horseflesh that was to be found in the Marquis's stables.

It was only a short distance to White's Club in St. James's Street, and the Marquis and Captain Collington entered through a door beside which stood the famous bow-window.

The window had been converted by Beau Brummel into a Holy of Holies and had become the centre of attraction for men in the fashionable world.

An ordinary member of the Club would as soon have thought of taking a seat on the Woolsack in the House of Lords as of appropriating one of the chairs in the sacred window.

In the previous year, however, Beau Brummel had indulged in an unfortunate and ruinous quarrel with his Patron and friend, the Prince Regent.

Socially that did not ruin him, since the Regent

had many enemies, and despite the fact that Beau
Brummel was barred from Carlton House Society continued to make much of him.

Financially, however, he was in an appalling state
of penury and early one day in 1816 he was forced to
flee from London to land in Calais without any re-
sources.

It was inevitable that as the Marquis and Charles
Collington walked into the Morning-Room at White's
they should think of Beau Brummel.

A large number of the friends who had been closest
to him were in the room and it was almost as if the
ghost of him—elegant, audacious and witty—was
amongst them.

The Marquis noticed Lord Alvanley, Prince Esterhazy and Lord Worcester, who were all listening to
the somewhat pontifical voice of Sir Algernon Gibbon.

When Sir Algernon saw the Marquis his face lit
up.

"Come and support me, Ruckley," he said. "I am
having an argument and I am certain you will be in
full agreement with my cause."

"Why should you be sure of that?" the Marquis
asked, sauntering towards the group standing round
the fire-place.

Sir Algernon Gibbon was, as everyone knew, attempting to take the place of Beau Brummel by setting himself up as an arbiter of fashion and deportment.

He was in fact, well qualified for the position,
having excellent taste both in furniture and in clothes.
He had also, since Beau Brummel's downfall, become
a close confidant and associate of the Regent.

He had, however, not the sharp perception nor the
impertinent self-confidence which had made Beau
Brummel so exceptional.

He was inclined to dogmatise and, although he was
very knowledgeable on the subjects about which he
spoke, his contemporaries were often more inclined
to laugh at him rather than accept his dictates.

"What I am saying," he said to the Marquis now, "is that it is impossible for someone who is ill-bred to disguise such a disadvantage of birth."

"And I am saying," Lord Alvanley interposed, "that if in particular a woman is well-educated and well instructed it would be quite easy for her to pass herself off as a Lady of Quality."

"She would not convince me," Sir Algernon said obstinately.

"This all started," Lord Worcester explained to the Marquis, "because Prince Esterhazy has queried the antecedents of a very pretty little French pigeon who swears she is an aristocratic refugee. She has a family tree—which she shows to her admiring gentlemen friends—which would make the Emperor Charlemagne's look like a piece of scrap-paper!"

"The whole thing is a complete fake!" Prince Esterhazy exclaimed.

"Of course it is!" Sir Algernon agreed. "And anyone with sensibility or taste is able at a glance to tell the dross from the gold—the fake from the real."

"What do you think, Ruckley?" Lord Alvanley enquired.

"I agree with you," the Marquis replied. "I am sure, if the lady in question was astute enough, she could easily convince the average man that she was who she pretended to be. Surely it is only a question of acting?"

"Well, I can tell you one thing," Sir Algernon said heatedly, "no woman or man would be able to deceive me. I can smell a *parvenu* a mile away!"

"Would you care to bet on it?" Lord Alvanley enquired.

"Of course," Sir Algernon answered.

"Why not?" Lord Worcester said. "We can all set ourselves to deceive Gibbon and make him eat his words. He is getting too pompous by half!"

Everyone laughed and Sir Algernon took it good-humouredly.

"All right," he said, "I will accept your bets. In fact

I will go further. I will make it worth your while. I will bet you one thousand guineas to a hundred that you will not find a man or woman who can convince me that they are blue-blooded when they are in fact exactly the opposite."

There was a roar of laughter from the gentlemen standing round him.

"Good for you, Gibbon!" Lord Worcester exclaimed. "I like a man who is prepared to back up his assertions in hard cash. What is more, I can do with some blunt at the moment!"

"Are foreigners barred?" Prince Esterhazy asked.

"No-one is barred," Sir Algernon declared. "But if you fail to deceive me, Gentlemen, then each failure will cost you fifty guineas! I promise you I shall be well in pocket before the year is out."

"I am not sure that he is not betting on a certainty," Captain Collington said in a low voice to the Marquis.

They were both aware that Sir Algernon was very astute, and he had made a fetish of good taste whether it concerned dress, deportment or the furniture which graced his houses.

He was wealthy because his mother had been an heiress, and his family tree, which dated back to Tudor times, was an example of how the great families of England inter-married amongst themselves.

Genealogy was Sir Algernon's main interest in life and the College of Heralds found him a continual thorn in their flesh as he frequently pointed out to them their mistakes.

Now Sir Algernon asked one of the stewards to bring him the Betting-Book.

Bound in leather and dating from 1743, the first record book having been destroyed in a fire several years earlier, it was an amazing record of the Members' personal interests.

The bets were entered in a very irregular manner, the writing showing all too clearly that a great number of the wagers had been made after dinner and entered by a hand that found it difficult to write clearly.

"Now how many of you are challenging me?" Sir Algernon enquired.

He sat down on a chair as he spoke and, putting the Betting-Book on a table in front of him, inscribed their names one after the other.

There were finally five—Prince Esterhazy, Lord Alvanley, Lord Worcester, Captain Collington and the Marquis.

"You have a year in which to confront me," Sir Algernon said. "If you have not been successful by that time in taking a thousand guineas from me, then I will give you all the best dinner that the Club can provide."

"Do not worry," the Prince said. "Long before that I shall be carrying your gold away in my pocket!"

"You are wrong," Lord Alvanley said, "I shall be the first to win because I need the money and therefore cannot wait!"

"Perhaps your luck will change tonight," the Prince answered, "in which case there will not be so much urgency where you are concerned."

Lord Alvanley needed luck, as the Prince well knew. His extravagance had ruined him, and he owed a gaming debt of £50,000.

Yet his courage, like his wit, never failed him, and he enjoyed all the year round a fresh apricot tart on his side-table at dinner.

Lord Worcester, son and heir of the Duke of Beaufort had recently spent a fortune he did not possess on a team of greys which he drove with a panache that excited public admiration.

His liaison with the famous Courtesan, Harriette Wilson, when he was still a minor had forced the Duke to offer her the sum of five hundred pounds a year for life.

When the Duke tried to settle her claim with a huge sum Harriette wrote her Memoirs, a *chronique scandaleuse* which set fashionable London in a turmoil.

Prince Esterhazy, on the other hand, was the Austrian Ambassador and a very wealthy man. On State occasions he was known to wear jewels worth eighty thousand pounds.

The gentlemen were joking with each other while Sir Algernon, having carefully recorded the conditions and date of the wager, set the Betting-Book on one side.

Charles Collington picked it up.

"You know," he said to the Marquis, "anyone reading this book in the future will think that most of the members of White's were half-witted. Look at this, for instance."

He pointed to a page on which was inscribed:

"Ld Lincoln bets Ld Winchelsea One Hundred Guineas to Fifty guineas that the Duchess Dowager of Marlborough does not survive the Duchess Dowager of Cleveland."

"I remember reading that entry," the Marquis said. "It is not as absurd as Lord Eglington's, who wagered he would find 'a man who shall kill twenty snipe in three-and-twenty shots.'"

"Where is that?" Charles Collington laughed.

"You will find it on one of the pages," the Marquis replied. "I once read the book through from cover to cover, and came to the conclusion that the majority of the bets were made either by drunks or lunatics."

"What about this one?" Charles Collington asked.

Turning the pages, he read aloud:

"Mr. Brummel bets Mr. Methuin two hundred guineas to twenty that Bonaparte will arrive in Paris on September 12th, 1812."

"At least Brummel collected on that occasion," the Marquis remarked.

"Poor Brummel, I wish he was here now," Charles Collington said. "If anyone could give an outsider a setdown it was he."

"That is true," the Marquis agreed. "Well, Charles, time is getting on. Shall we proceed to the Opera House?"

To his surprise his friend did not answer. Then after a moment Captain Collington said in a strange voice:

"Look at this, Fabius."

He passed the book to the Marquis and, following the direction of his finger, the Marquis read:

"Mr. Jethro Ruck bets Sir James Copley that he will be in possession of a fortune and a title by the end of the year 1818."

The Marquis read it slowly then he turned to look at his friend.

"That gives you exactly eight months," Charles Collington said quietly.

"Do you really think—you cannot believe—" the Marquis began.

"Do not be a fool, Fabius. It is quite obvious. I told you Jethro has been praying for your death, and I am quite certain that tonight he was doing something a little more active than pray!"

"I have a feeling you are right," the Marquis agreed.

"What are you going to do about it?" Charles Collington enquired.

The Marquis shrugged his shoulders.

"What can I do? I can hardly accuse Jethro of throwing masonry at me from the top of my house unless I have proof."

"But good Lord, Fabius, you cannot just sit and do nothing! He will get to you sooner or later."

"That is rather a challenge, is it not?"

"Now do not be turnip-headed about this," Charles Collington admonished. "I have always detested your cousin, as you well know. I have always known that he is an unmitigated blackguard and it is no surprise

14

to me that he plans to murder you. The only thing is
—I could not bear him to be successful."

"I do not particularly care for the idea myself!"
the Marquis said dryly.

"Then do something about it," Charles Collington
said urgently.

"What do you suggest?"

"There must be something!"

"There is," the Marquis said slowly, but he did not,
in spite of his friend's curiosity, volunteer what that
might be.

The following afternoon Lady Walden, at her house
near St. Albans in Hertfordshire, was surprised to receive a visitor.

"Fabius!" she exclaimed in surprise when the Marquis was announced. "I thought you never came to the
country once you had left it for the London Season."

"I wanted to see you," the Marquis replied.

"I am flattered," Lady Walden smiled, "but as it
happens I am leaving here tomorrow, for I do not intend to miss the Duchess of Devonshire's Ball which
takes place on Thursday."

"I was sure you would be there," the Marquis said.

"And yet you have come all this way to see me today. I am flattered, Fabius."

There was, however, surprise in her beautiful eyes
as she looked at him.

Eurydice Walden had been the toast of St. James
ever since she emerged from the school-room six years
earlier.

She was lovely in the manner of the fashionable
beauties of the time, with fair hair, blue eyes and an
exquisitely curved body which left no-one in any
doubt as to her femininity.

She had been fêted for her beauty when she had
burst almost like a comet on the astonished Social
World, but she was at the moment even more desirable because as her beauty had increased with the
years so had her assets.

She had married at seventeen the wild, attractive and immensely wealthy Sir Beaugrave Walden.

He had, however, been killed in the last month of the war, leaving an immense fortune to his widow who, a year later on the death of her father, inherited together with other assets ten thousand acres of land which marched with the Marquis's own Estate.

Eurydice and the Marquis had known each other since they were children, and it had always been understood between their fathers that they should be married and their estates united.

The Marquis, however, had been abroad with his Regiment in Portugal when Eurydice married, and although his father bewailed the fact, he himself had felt no particular loss.

He sat down now on an elegant damask sofa in Eurydice's Drawing-Room and regarded her with a scrutinising expression which she found somehow perplexing.

"What is the matter, Fabius? You appear worried."

She was in fact puzzling her head as to why he should call on her so unexpectedly.

She was glad that she was wearing one of her prettiest muslin gowns because, although she was not strongly interested personally in the man she had known ever since childhood, she was well aware that he was sought after by the majority of her female friends.

To capture his interest would be a feather in her cap, for which she would undoubtedly be envied.

"I want to talk to you, Eurydice."

"You said that before."

"I know, but I am not quite certain how to explain to you why I am here."

"It is unlike you to be so reticent," Eurydice teased.

"What I have come to say," the Marquis went on in a serious tone, "is that I think we should do what was always expected of us by your father and by mine."

16

"What was that?" Eurydice enquired.

There was a note of astonishment in her voice. She could hardly believe that the Marquis was in fact going to say, what she half suspected trembled on his lips.

"I think we should get married!"

"Are you serious?" Eurydice enquired.

"Very serious," he answered. "You know as well as I do that it was what our fathers planned since the moment you were born. They were close friends, and they both envisaged the day would come when our Estates would become one because you became my wife."

"But all that was years ago," Eurydice objected, "and now they are both dead."

"But we are alive," the Marquis said, "and I cannot help feeling it was an eminently sensible plan."

"Sensible perhaps, but not very romantic."

"I am sorry if I have expressed myself badly," the Marquis said with a smile most women found irresistible. "I am very fond of you, Eurydice, as you should well know. I always have been."

"That is nonsense!" Eurydice retorted rudely. "You heartily disliked me when you were a small boy!"

"I am sure I did nothing of the sort!"

"You always said you had no use for girls. You used to pull my hair at parties and once when I threw your cricket ball away you actually hit me."

"Good God, Eurydice," the Marquis exclaimed, "you can hardly hold that against me now!"

"Why not? After all, you have not fallen over yourself to show your affection since we have grown up."

"Have I had a chance?" the Marquis asked. "You were married while I was away fighting in Portugal."

"You certainly did not seem very perturbed about it when we did meet!"

"I only saw you perhaps once or twice after you were married," the Marquis said. "Besides Beaugrave was a friend of mine. You could hardly expect me to make love to you under his nose."

"You did not want to make love to me," Eurydice retorted. "You never have wanted to, so why should you now wish to marry me?"

"For one thing, I think it is time I got married," the Marquis said, "and for another, I am quite certain we should deal well together. I would look after you, Eurydice, and you cannot go on getting yourself gossiped about forever!"

"Gossiped about? And who is slandering me I should like to know?"

"Now really!" the Marquis exclaimed with a hint of amusement in his voice. "You know quite well that you have caused one scandal after another ever since you have been widowed. And as if you did not know, everyone in London is now talking about you and Severn."

There was a pause. Then casting down her eyes Eurydice said:

"Perhaps with reason!"

"Good God!" the Marquis exclaimed, "do you mean to say the Duke has come up to scratch?"

"I am not answering that question," Eurydice replied with dignity.

"Then he has not!" the Marquis said shrewdly.

"You have no right to come here and cross-question me."

The Marquis rose to his feet.

"I see it all now," he said. "You came down here in the middle of the Season, which I thought was strange, simply because you believed the Duke would follow you. Well, has he?"

"I told you, Fabius, it is none of your business!" Eurydice cried. "Go away and leave me alone."

"I came here to ask you if you would marry me," the Marquis said firmly. "You have not yet given me your answer."

"I need time to think about it."

He looked at her speculatively and the expression in his eyes was hard.

"In other words," he said slowly, "you are waiting

18

to see if Severn makes you a better offer. If he does you will accept. If not, a Marquis is quite a good catch!"

"There are dozens of people who want to marry me," Eurydice asserted rudely, rather like a small girl who wishes to be aggressive.

"I am well aware of that!" the Marquis replied, "but I doubt, apart from myself and Severn, if you would be prepared to accept any of those love-lorn swain who write odes to your lips and leave little *billets-doux* on your doorstep every morning. It is doubtful if the majority could afford to do anything else."

He spoke sarcastically and Eurydice, rising, stamped her foot.

"How dare you speak to me like that, Fabius!" she said. "You always have been odious and I hate you! Do you understand? I hate you!"

"Nevertheless you will marry me," the Marquis remarked.

"I shall do nothing of the sort," she retorted. "I have no wish to marry anyone unless . . ."

She paused.

". . . unless they can give you the position that you want in Society," the Marquis finished. "You have enough money, Eurydice, we are both aware of that, but you want the standing. You want to be a great Hostess. It was always your ambition."

She did not reply and after a moment he went on:

"That narrows the field, does it not? In fact, as I have already said, it leaves Severn in the lead and me a close second. There is no-one else in the race."

"I am not going to answer you," Eurydice snapped.

The Marquis was aware that she was almost shaking with rage.

"Well I would like an answer soon, in fact within two or three days," the Marquis said. "It is a matter of some urgency."

"What do you mean by that?" Eurydice asked curiously. "Why should you suddenly be in such a hurry?"

Then she gave an exclamation.

"I know why you want to get married! I am not a fool, Fabius. It is because of Jethro, is it not?"

"It is now my turn not to answer questions," the Marquis replied.

"But I will answer them for you," Eurydice said. "The whole world and his wife are well aware that Jethro is waiting to step into your shoes. He is banking on it. He was quite certain you would be killed like poor Beaugrave, and when you were not, he has boasted, when he is in his cups—which is most of the time—that he will get rid of you somehow!"

She paused.

"That is true, is it not?"

"Perhaps," the Marquis admitted.

"So you want a wife and you want an heir," Eurydice said almost beneath her breath.

"Well?" the Marquis enquired.

"I suppose if I say no you will find someone else to marry you. Any wife, whatever she is like, will be better than thinking of Jethro setting himself up at Ruckley and sporting a coronet in the House of Lords."

"You express yourself very eloquently," the Marquis said. "I am waiting for an answer, Eurydice."

"I am not going to give you one at the moment."

"So we have to wait for Severn?"

"Per . . . haps."

"Has he given you any intimation as to whether his feelings for you are serious?"

"I do not wish to discuss him with you," Eurydice said. "In fact I have nothing more to say at the moment, Fabius, except that I will consider your offer of marriage. It is of course very flattering!"

She spoke sarcastically, and quite suddenly the Marquis smiled.

"This is not the way I had intended to approach you."

"No?"

"I meant to doll it up with roses and blue ribbons. It is just that I am not very good at that sort of thing."

"I have heard very different accounts from the ladies upon whom you have bestowed your favours!"

"That is rather different."

"Is it impossible to think of love and marriage at the same time?" Eurydice asked in a low voice.

"Not impossible," the Marquis admitted, "but impracticable. You know as well as I do Eurydice, that life is not like a romantic novelette."

"I loved Beaugrave . . . I loved him madly!"

"That was perhaps the exception which proves the rule," the Marquis agreed. "But do you think your love, your infatuation, or whatever it was, would have lasted? We both know what Beaugrave was like."

Eurydice was silent. She was thinking of the wild, raffish young man she had married. They had both been little more than children and their life together had been one escapade after another.

Then because he craved more excitement than she could provide for him, Beaugrave Walden had bought himself into a fashionable Cavalry Regiment and been killed within six months of joining.

"You see," the Marquis said quietly, as if he followed her thoughts, "a sensible marriage could give you security and a husband who will look after you and protect you. I will do that, Eurydice."

"I believe you would," she answered suddenly serious. "At the same time, have you never loved anyone, Fabius, enough to wish to marry her?"

"The answer is no."

"But you have had many love affairs?"

"Not as many as I am credited with," the Marquis answered, "but enough, Eurydice, to know that what people call 'love' is an ephemeral experience which seldom lasts."

"Is that really true?" she questioned.

She walked away from him to look out on the sunlit garden. There were daffodils under the trees and the shrubs were coming into bloom.

She looked very lovely silhouetted against the dark green of the trees outside, and the Marquis, as his eyes rested on her golden hair and clear-cut features, was suddenly perceptive enough to realise that Eurydice would never be content with no more than a great position, however important it might be.

Like all women, she wanted love, a love that was more than passion, more than desire, a love which he knew he was incapable of giving her.

As if her thoughts had brought her some solution to the problems that beset her, Eurydice turned from the window.

"You are right, Fabius," she said. "I do need security, and I intend to wait to hear what the Duke has to say to me tonight."

"Tonight?" the Marquis asked.

"He is coming to dinner."

"In which case I can most certainly wait until tomorrow."

"I may not be able to give you an answer even then," Eurydice said. "The trouble is, Fabius, I do not want to marry you. If I cannot be a Duchess, I want to be in love."

"You are crying for the moon," the Marquis said.

"How I should like to prove that you are wrong," Eurydice retorted almost rudely. "You are so insufferably sure of yourself."

The Marquis laughed.

"I see it is high time I left you," he said. "Besides, you will want to make yourself particularly alluring for this evening."

There was something almost jeering in the way he spoke the words, and Eurydice, tossing her head, walked towards the door.

"I shall not try to persuade you to stay," she said. "Perhaps when you next call on me either here or in London you will be in a more agreeable mood."

"Or perhaps a more amorous one," the Marquis said. "Would you like to kiss me good-bye, Eurydice?"

"I can think of nothing I wish to do less," she retorted, and opened the door before he could do so.

"Good-bye, Fabius," she said. "You annoy me. You

always have annoyed me. I can only hope that one day you will find someone who will make you suffer all the tortures of hell. It will be so very good for you!"

"Your solicitude overwhelms me!" the Marquis retorted.

Then he stepped outside Eurydice's very impressive house on which her father had expended an exorbitant amount of money, and climbed into his Phaeton.

He had driven down from London with only a small groom seated beside him and now, as he took up the reins, the boy released the horses' bridles and, as the Marquis started off, he clambered like a small monkey into his seat at the back of the Phaeton.

They drove away down the drive.

As they went the Marquis had a great desire to reach Ruckley as quickly as possible.

He suddenly felt appalled at what he had done—proposed marriage for the first time in his life—and to someone who said quite frankly that she disliked him.

It had seemed last night and again this morning to be an eminently sensible action to invite Eurydice to be his wife.

He thought that he could do no better than fulfil what had been his father's hopes, and to rely on his father's judgment. But now he felt horrified at the step he had taken.

Life would be intolerable with Eurydice, taunting him at every turn, yearning for affection he was incapable of giving her, and taking every opportunity of irritating him because she felt piqued by his indifference.

The Marquis was very experienced where women were concerned, and he was well aware that they could make life extremely uncomfortable simply because they felt they had been slighted.

Many of his love affairs had in fact ended unpleasantly simply because a woman had been so very much

23

more in love with him that he had pretended to be
with her.

It was, he was well aware, something that a female
found impossible to forgive. That she should lay down
her heart for a man to walk on, and he should in fact
be immune to every wile and trick with which she
had contrived to capture him.

'One cannot fall in love to order,' the Marquis
thought almost despairingly.

Then, as he thought it, he realised what a fool he
had been to think that Eurydice would not realise
immediately that he was simply making use of her.

Yet he could not pretend to love her and he had
the feeling he had made a mess of his first proposal
of marriage.

Because it made him angry to realise not only that
he had made a fool of himself, but also that if the
Duke did not come up to scratch there was every
chance that Eurydice might accept his offer, he
pushed his horses.

He was a magnificent driver—a Corinthian—and
was known to be able to control even the wildest or
most difficult animal.

Now, because he was in a rage, he took his team
of four down the road which lay between the two
Estates at a pace which would have made his Head-
Groom look at him in surprise.

The horses swung through the gates at Ruckley
and proceeded up the oak avenue in a manner which
made the fragile Phaeton seem almost to fly through
the air.

They swept up a short incline beyond which there
was a sharp descent into the valley, where Ruckley
House stood. As the Marquis reached the top of the
rise he suddenly saw standing on the drive in front
of him a lone figure.

It was a woman with her back to him.

Because he was moving so fast, there was nothing
he could do but attempt to turn the horses at the
very last moment and drag them onto the verge.

He pulled sharply on the reins, shouting to the woman as he did so to get out of the way.

The horses were almost upon her as she turned a surprised face in their direction.

Then even as the Marquis with a superb effort pulled the horses clear of her, she slipped as she turned and the wheel caught her.

The Marquis drew his horses to a standstill and looked back to see a woman's body lying on the ground behind him.

"Oh, God!" he exclaimed. "I must have killed her!"

Chapter Two

The groom ran to the horses' heads while the Marquis jumped down and hurried up the drive to where the fallen woman sprawled limply on the ground.

When he reached her he saw that she was very young. The wheel had caught her on the left side. There was blood on her forehead and the white blouse she was wearing had been torn from her shoulder where the skin was gashed and bleeding profusely.

The Marquis bent down, taking his handkerchief from his coat pocket as he did so. Then realising that the girl was unconscious, he looked around first at his Phaeton and then at the distance to the house. He decided he would carry her.

Vaguely at the back of his mind he remembered that it was dangerous if someone was hurt internally for them to be jolted or even moved, but he could not leave her lying injured on the drive.

She was small and slight and it would obviously be less disturbing if he carried her than if he attempted to drive her in the Phaeton.

Very gently he lifted the recumbent figure in his arms. She was very light.

"Drive the horses home, Jim," he ordered his groom who was watching from the Phaeton. "Tell them at the house that there has been an accident."

"Very good, M'Lord," the groom answered and set off down the drive.

Moving slowly the Marquis followed.

As he walked he looked down at his burden and realised that apart from the bleeding wound on her forehead, she was lovely, but in a strange manner.

She had black hair, so long that the Marquis was certain that when she was standing it would reach below her waist and her closed eyes were perfect half-crescents with long lashes dark against an ivory skin.

She did not look English; then glancing at her clothes the Marquis understood.

The girl he had knocked down was a Gypsy!

There was no mistaking the full red skirt worn, he was sure, over a number of others, the black velvet bodice laced in the front, the sash around her small waist, and the embroidered blouse, low at the neck, leaving the arms bare.

He had always supposed that Gypsies were dirty, but the girl he held in his arms was exquisitely clean, and there was a faint fragrance of some Oriental perfume which seemed to come from her hair.

The Marquis saw that round her neck she wore a necklace of gold coins linked together with what appeared to be small pieces of red glass.

Gypsy women liked jewellery, he remembered hearing at some time or another.

He had an idea that some of the coins the girl wore were of great antiquity. They were certainly old and all of them were foreign. Then he chided himself for being interested in anything except his victim who might in fact be badly injured.

She was certainly not dead, which was one consolation. She was unconscious, but she was breathing evenly and her rather frightening pallor might well, he thought, be habitual.

It did not take him long to traverse the drive and reach the court-yard which lay in front of a great flight of steps leading to the main entrance.

As he drew nearer a number of men-servants came hurrying towards him.

Bush, the Butler, reached him first.

28

"We heard there'd been an accident, M'Lord. Is the lady badly hurt?"

"I have no idea," the Marquis answered curtly.

Then as he moved on with the Butler beside him, the latter exclaimed:

"It's no lady, M'Lord! She's one of them Gypsies!"

"What Gypsies?"

"There are always some of them in the woods at this time of the year, M'Lord."

The Marquis walked up the steps.

There appeared to be quite a number of people in the Marble Hall when he entered, but he ignored them and climbed the carved staircase to where on the first landing he found Mrs. Meedham, the Housekeeper, agitatedly bobbing a curtsy at the sight of him.

"Which bed-room is ready?" the Marquis enquired.

"All of them, M'Lord."

Then she looked at the unconscious figure in the arms of the Marquis and exclaimed:

"Why, it's one of them Gypsies! A room in the servants' wing will do for her, M'Lord."

The Marquis walked across the landing.

"Open the door," he said briefly.

After a moment's surprise Mrs. Meedham obeyed him, and he entered one of the large State-Rooms which opened off the first-floor landing.

"But surely, M'Lord . . ." Mrs. Meedham protested, only to be silenced as the Marquis said:

"There could be a risk, Mrs. Meedham, in carrying this young woman any further. Her life may be in danger."

He moved towards the big four-poster bed but Mrs. Meedham hurried after him.

"Not on the cover, M'Lord! The sheets can be washed."

She pulled back the embroidered silk and opened the bed-clothes as she spoke.

Very gently the Marquis set down the girl he carried on the white linen sheets embroidered with the Ruckley crest surmounted by a coronet.

Her head fell back against the pillows, and her hair was jet black in contrast to the white linen.

"Send for Hobley," the Marquis ordered.

"I'm here, M'Lord."

A middle-aged man came hurrying into the room.

Hobley had been at Ruckley House ever since the Marquis could remember. Officially he was his Lordship's Valet, but he was famous for his skill in being able to set bones.

He had in fact set the Marquis's own collar-bone on one occasion and, if anyone on the Estate broke a leg or an arm, it was always Hobley who attended them.

He was far more efficient, far more knowledgeable than any local Physician, and in fact everyone asked for him whatever their injury.

Hobley moved to the bed-side now, looked at the cut on the unconscious girl's forehead and the bleeding wounds on her arm. He then noticed there was blood dripping from beneath her skirts and pulled them aside to show a deep cut on one ankle.

As he did so, the Marquis saw the girl's legs were bare although she wore red slippers cut low and ornamented with little buckles of silver.

"Hot water and bandages, if you please," Hobley demanded, and Mrs. Meedham and several house-maids who were congregated round the door hurried to fetch what he required.

"Are there any bones broken?" the Marquis asked.

"I can't tell as yet, M'Lord," Hobley answered. "Did the wheel pass over her?"

"I cannot be sure," the Marquis replied. "It happened so quickly."

He paused and added:

"It was my fault, Hobley. I was driving too fast."

" 'Tis not often you have an accident, M'Lord," Hobley said, and added reassuringly: "I've an idea this is not as bad as it looks!"

"But she is unconscious."

"That is because of the wound on her head," Hobley replied. "Leave her with me, M'Lord. I'll find out what is wrong and let Your Lordship know if it is necessary to send for the Doctor."

"Thank you, Hobley," the Marquis said with a note of relief in his voice.

He left the room.

As he crossed the landing it was to see Mrs. Meedham and the house-maids hurrying down the passage carrying jugs of water, bandages and towels in their hands.

He went downstairs and, ignoring the Salon where he knew the Butler would have laid out wine and refreshments, he walked instead down the passage which led to the Library.

One of the most impressive rooms in the house, it had been completely renovated in his father's time, who had also added two or three thousand volumes to the books already collected by his grand-father.

Seated at a desk in the centre of the Library was an elderly man with white hair.

He looked up indifferently as the Marquis opened the door, then rose with an exclamation of surprise and pleasure.

"I was not expecting you, My Lord. Why did no-one tell me you were coming?"

"It is a surprise," the Marquis said. "I only decided last night it was necessary for me to visit the country."

He was speaking to the man who had been his Tutor, friend and companion for many years.

The Reverend Horace Redditch had been employed by the late Marquis to tutor his son before he went to Eton.

He had fitted in so well and been so liked by the whole family that in time he became the Marquis's personal Chaplain, as well as being Librarian and Curator.

He was known by everyone in the House and on the Estate as "The Reverend," and enjoyed the familiarity which made it a term of affection.

He had accompanied the present Marquis as a

31

young man on many visits around the country. They had once spent a delightful holiday in Ireland combining learning with the pleasure of salmon fishing.

"It is nice to see you, Sir," the Marquis said, with a note of affection in his voice which few people evoked from him.

"Are you enjoying London?" The Reverend enquired.

"Not particularly!" the Marquis admitted. "As a matter of fact I have just had an accident. I knocked down a Gypsy girl. She is upstairs and Hobley is attending to her."

"A Gypsy?" The Reverend repeated. "Well, that is not surprising. It is the time of year when they visit us."

"Tell me about them," the Marquis said.

"It was your grand-mother, I believe, who gave them permission to camp on the Estate. She was always sorry for everyone who was homeless and I think too she was very interested in Gypsy people who wander over the earth with no settled abode."

"I really know very little about them," the Marquis said.

"They came originally from India," The Reverend replied. "Which of course accounts for their dark hair and dark skins."

"And they have been nomads ever since?"

"There are of course numerous legends and explanations as to why they can never settle down."

"Are there many Gypsies in England?"

"Quite a number, I believe," The Reverend replied. "But they are to be found in every country. If you are interested I must see if we have any books about them."

The Marquis shrugged his shoulders.

"I seem to remember that the Game-keepers dislike them, thinking that they poach the pheasants."

"It has been a tradition on this Estate that they should not be harassed or driven away," The Rever-

end said, "and as I think there is something pic-
turesque about them, I hope you will not refuse them
the hospitality which they have found at Ruckley for
nearly a century."

"I will certainly not do that!" the Marquis said. "After all, I feel responsible for the girl I have just injured. Do you think I should get in touch with her
tribe, or whatever they call themselves?"

"Maybe she is not as badly hurt as you suspect,"
The Reverend said soothingly. "Anyway Hobley will
deal with it."

"Yes, I am sure he will," the Marquis replied.

He talked for a little while longer to his old Tutor,
then went into the Salon to find as he had expected
there was wine and a whole assortment of sandwiches
and other delicacies laid out on a silver tray.

The Marquis had stopped for luncheon at an Inn
on his way down from London before he had called
on Eurydice. So, while he sipped a glass of excellent
wine from his cellars, he was in fact not hungry.

He had only been in the Salon a short while before
Hobley came to find him.

"How is she?" the Marquis asked.

"There're no bones broken, M'Lord, but the blow on
the head has undoubtedly caused concussion. I should
not be surprised if tonight she runs a fever!"

"It is not serious?" the Marquis asked.

"No, M'Lord, the cuts and bruises are only super-
ficial, and when the Gypsy regains consciousness we
shall know how much she has been affected in the
head."

"Then she must stay here until she is better," the
Marquis said.

"Mrs. Meedham is anxious to move her to another
part of the house, M'Lord. She feels it is unseemly that
a Gypsy should occupy one of the State bed-rooms."

"Seemly or not, she is to remain where she is," the
Marquis said sharply. "It is my fault the girl was hurt
and I will have her treated with all possible considera-

tion. Make that clear, Hobley, to the rest of the staff."

"I will, M'Lord, but Your Lordship understands they are afraid of Gypsies."

"Why are they afraid?" the Marquis asked.

"They fear they might put the 'Evil Eye' upon them, steal their children or curse them."

The Marquis laughed.

"All the more reason for them to be polite to our guest! She does not seem to me a kind of creature who would curse anybody."

He thought as he spoke of how light the girl had been as he carried her in his arms, and it seemed to him, although he might have imagined it, that the strange fragrance from her hair still lingered on his coat.

"Well, if there is nothing more I can do, Hobley," he said, "I am returning to London."

"We thought you might do so, M'Lord. The horses have been changed and are ready the moment Your Lordship asks for them."

"Then have them brought round," the Marquis said, "and when our guest is ready to depart, see that she is recompensed for the damage I have inflicted on her."

"What would you consider a reasonable sum, M'Lord?" Hobley asked respectfully.

The Marquis considered a moment.

"I should think about five pounds would cover it, Hobley. Ask Mr. Graystone for the money."

"I will, M'Lord. When shall we see Your Lordship again?"

"I have no idea," the Marquis replied. "The Season is at its height, Hobley, and I am sure you would not wish me to miss any of the endless extravagant and exhausting entertainments which take place night after night."

The Marquis spoke sarcastically, then smiled almost apologetically at the old servant who he knew had loved him since he was a child.

"Anything wrong, Master Fabius?" Hobley asked.

It was a question that seemed to the Marquis to

have echoed all down the years. It was always Hobley who had understood if things went awry or if he was upset.

"No, Hobley, not really," he said quietly. "It is just that Captain Collington and I were saying only last night we are getting older. Things do not seem as amusing as they were when I was young."

"You're still young enough to enjoy yourself, M'Lord," Hobley said with a twinkle in his eye, "and if Your Lordship takes my advice you won't waste one minute of the years as they pass."

"Are you having regrets about your own lost youth?" the Marquis enquired.

"No, M'Lord, I've no regrets, and that's something I pray that Your Lordship'll never have. In my experience there's always something to look forward to and there's always adventures when we least expect them."

"You have cheered me up, Hobley!"

The Marquis was smiling as he walked across the Hall and ordered his Phaeton to be brought round immediately.

No-one was more surprised than the Marquis to find himself a week later travelling the same road from London to call on Eurydice.

He had expected to see her at the Duchess of Devonshire's Ball, and he had searched for her during the next four nights at Assemblies, Balls and dinner parties given by their mutual friends, to which he was quite sure she had been invited.

But there was no sign of her and, as the Duke of Severn was also missing, it was not difficult to imagine where they could both be found.

He had confided to no-one that he was waiting for Eurydice's answer to his proposal of marriage, but his friend, Charles Collington, was aware that he was restless and unusually inattentive and uninterested in the succession of parties they attended.

"What is the matter, Fabius?" he asked. "You are like a bear with a sore head!"

"I will tell you about it later," the Marquis promised.

"Jethro has not been up to his tricks again?" Charles asked suspiciously.

"If he has, it was as ineffectual as the falling masonry from my roof!" the Marquis said.

"I hardly think that is a joking matter," Charles Collington replied severely.

"As a matter of fact it is not," the Marquis said. "I had the roof inspected the following day and the stonemason I employed informed me that it was quite impossible for such a large piece of the parapet to have broken away accidentally."

"You mean—as we suspected—it was deliberate?" Charles Collington asked incredulously.

"I was thinking," the Marquis said, "how it would have been quite easy for someone to have hidden in the garden in the centre of the Square. Then when I appeared in the doorway—with the lights behind me—they had only to signal to whoever was on the roof."

"That of course is exactly what happened!" Charles Collington exclaimed. "It was just fortunate that you turned back to speak to Burton."

"Very fortunate!" the Marquis agreed.

"Well, for God's sake—be careful!"

"How can I?" the Marquis asked irritably. "If I have to go about with an armed guard, stay at home, or live eternally on the alert expecting to be poisoned, shot at or struck to the ground—all I can say is—let Jethro try and get it over!"

"If we had taken up that attitude where Bonaparte was concerned, we would have lost the war!"

The Marquis was about to make some quite heated reply, when he burst out laughing.

"I cannot allow you, Charles," he said, "to compare Jethro with Napoleon! It is giving him an undue importance!"

"I never thought it mattered if a man was impor-

tant or not, if it was his gun which blew a piece of
lead through me," Charles Collington retorted, and
for a moment the Marquis had no reply.

Driving to the country now, he thought he had
taken an unwise step in his effort to circumvent Jethro's plan for securing the inheritance for himself.

He knew, if he was honest with himself, that he
did not really wish to marry Eurydice.

In theory it had seemed a good idea. In practice
he knew they had no chance of real happiness together and little hope of even getting on reasonably
well.

He was quite sure that the reason Eurydice had sent
for him was to tell him that Severn had not proposed
as she had expected, and she was therefore willing to
become the Marchioness of Ruckley.

It had seemed, as he had told her, a practical and
sensible idea and one that could be a surprise to
neither of them.

But when he thought of Eurydice being permanently
at his side either in London or at Ruckley House,
the Marquis knew that never had his freedom seemed
more attractive.

However what had been done could not be un-
done. He had offered Eurydice marriage, and if she
accepted him he must put a good face on it.

It was with a sense of depression and an ominous
feeling of foreboding that the Marquis stepped down
outside the pillared portico of Eurydice's house and
was ushered with due ceremony into the Drawing-
Room where she was waiting for him.

He could not help appreciating that she was looking
exceedingly lovely. The sunshine haloed her fair hair
as she turned from the window and as she moved towards him with a smile he thought he had never seen
her face more radiant.

"You have come, Fabius! I am so glad to see you!"

The Marquis raised her hand to his lips.

"I am honoured by such a warm welcome," he said
in his deep voice.

"You must forgive me for dragging you away from London for the second time," Eurydice said, "but what I have to say is of the utmost importance."

The Marquis drew in his breath and waited for the blow to fall.

"Shall we sit down?" Eurydice suggested.

She indicated a chair with her hand and as the Marquis settled himself she sat down on the sofa.

"I have much to tell you, Fabius, but I will start with what is most important to you."

The Marquis nodded his head.

His eyes were on her face and he thought that she was in fact in a completely different mood from the one in which he had last seen her.

"I have first to ask you," Eurydice said, "if you will take over this Estate and run it with your own?"

"But of course. That is understood," the Marquis replied. "It would be a waste of time and money for us both to employ separate Managers, Overseers and Agents. It will just be a question of which of our employees are the most dependable."

Eurydice smiled.

"What I am really saying, perhaps not very clearly, is that later I may sell you the Estate, but at the moment I would rather that you ran it for me. You can rent it if you would prefer."

The Marquis looked at her in a puzzled way.

"I do not understand."

"Why should you?" Eurydice asked and she gave a little sigh.

It seemed to be an expression of almost rapturous satisfaction.

"I am going away, Fabius, and I cannot just leave the Estate with no-one to look after it. It would seem a betrayal of my home."

"Going away?" the Marquis repeated. "Are you telling me that you have accepted Severn?"

"No, I refused him."

The Marquis was very still.

"Then ..."

"I am to be married," Eurydice said quickly, "but not to the Duke, nor to you."

"There is someone else?" the Marquis asked incredulously, "but who?"

"Someone of whom you have never heard," Eurydice replied. "His name is Silas Wingdale."

The Marquis raised his eyebrows.

"Silas Wingdale?" he repeated. "Who the devil is he?"

Eurydice jumped to her feet and she was laughing.

"I thought you would be astonished," she said. "He is an American. He lives in Virginia and I love him! Yes, I love him! And so I am going to marry him, Fabius."

"Are you telling me the truth?" the Marquis asked in astonishment.

"I do not care a fig for the Ducal strawberry leaves or the Ruckley diamonds or any of the things you thought were so important to me," Eurydice said in an ecstatic voice. "I am in love as I have never been in love for years! Not since I first knew poor Beaugrave. But this is different! Silas is older and he loves me in a very different way. In fact being with him is like reaching Heaven itself!"

The Marquis put his hand up to his forehead.

"Are you quite certain this is not just a joke?" he asked. "You are serious, Eurydice?"

"I have never been more serious in my life," she answered. "Silas and I are to be married quietly tomorrow morning and then we are taking a ship to America from Plymouth and Heaven knows if I shall ever return to this country."

"Do you know what you are letting yourself in for, or the sort of place where you are going to live?" the Marquis asked.

"I have seen sketches of Silas's house and it is delightful. Very like a large English manor, for that matter. But it would not matter to me if he lived in a

39

shack. I love him, Fabius, and he loves me! That is more important than anything else . . . but I have only just realised it!"

It was an hour later that the Marquis, still feeling bemused and astonished by what he had heard, drove his horses to his own house.

He could hardly credit that anyone, least of all Eurydice, would throw up everything which before had seemed important in life to set off across the ocean with a man of whom she knew little, though in her eyes he seemed endowed with all the virtues.

The Marquis had in fact argued with her, and asked her at least to delay her marriage and her departure until her friends had a chance to meet Silas Wingdale.

"It would not matter what you said about him so why should I delay my marriage?" Eurydice asked, with a touch of her old aggressiveness. "I am not asking you to marry him, Fabius, so whatever your opinion might be, it is of no consequence."

Then she had reached up her hand to touch the Marquis's cheek.

"When you fall in love, as you undoubtedly will one day," she said softly, "you will understand why there are no arguments that could change my mind, and nothing that anyone could say would influence me. It is Silas I want and Silas I intend to have."

Eurydice had spoken with such warmth that the Marquis realised she was a very different person from the hard, scheming young woman she had become after her husband's death.

He had thought she was out only for social advancement and for making herself the most notorious and the most talked about figure in the *Beau Monde*.

It was astonishing that she could have changed so quickly from a determined schemer into a gentle, feminine creature whose eyes shone and who seemed to glow at the mere mention of the name of the man with whom she was in love.

'Dammit,' the Marquis thought, as he drove down

the drive towards Ruckley House, 'why cannot I feel like that?'

Then he laughed at himself for imagining that such a thing was possible.

The servants were surprised to see him.

"This is a pleasure, M'Lord," the Butler said, hurrying into the Hall.

"Where is Hobley?" the Marquis enquired.

"I'll send for him, M'Lord. The Reverend's in the Library."

"Then I will go and talk to him."

The Marquis opened the door of the Library and saw that his Tutor was not, as he had expected, sitting at the big desk in the centre of the room, but that standing at a bookcase was a slim figure he had seen once before.

She turned round to face him, and his first impression was that her eyes were far too big for her face.

Fringed by the dark lashes he had noticed before, they were very unusual eyes but only as he drew nearer did he realise that while the pupils seemed unnaturally large, the colour of the Gypsy's eyes was not black, as he might have expected, but a very dark green.

She did not speak, but waited as the Marquis advanced towards her. When he reached her he held out his hand.

"I am the Marquis of Ruckley and I owe you an apology."

Almost reluctantly it seemed to him she laid her fingers in his.

They were cool and as he held them for a moment he had the unaccountable feeling that some strange vibration passed between them.

"You are better?" he asked.

"I have recovered, thank you."

The voice was low and musical with a faint foreign accent.

The Marquis glanced at her forehead.

The wound where the wheel of the Phaeton had hit her was still red, and the skin around it was discoloured the purple and orange of a deep bruise.

She was wearing the same attractive Gypsy dress that she had done when he first saw her, but he could see that the blouse was not the one which had been torn from her shoulder. On her arm he could see a bandage.

"I need not tell you how sorry I am that I should have hurt you," the Marquis said.

"It was my fault," the Gypsy answered. "I was looking at your house and I forgot everything else because it was so beautiful."

"I am glad you think so," the Marquis replied. "As I expect someone has told you, it was built in the reign of Queen Elizabeth and there are very few Tudor houses in the whole country to equal it."

There was a note of pride in his voice because Ruckley had always meant so much to him.

"I did not think English houses would be as fine as they are," the Gypsy said.

"You sound as if you have not been in England long."

"No, this is the first time."

"What is your name?"

"Saviya."

"That is a very unusual name."

"It may seem so to you," she replied, "but it is quite a common name amongst my tribe."

"And what is that?" the Marquis enquired.

He thought for a moment she would not answer him. Then she said:

"We are the Kalderash."

She saw that he was ignorant of what this meant and she added:

"The metal-workers, the farriers, the healers, the musicians and the magicians!"

"Magicians?" the Marquis exclaimed, then added: "Oh, you mean fortune-telling and that sort of thing. I believe the Gypsies are very good at that!"

42

Saviya gave him a faint smile that had a hint of mockery in it before she said in a low voice:

"I must thank you, My Lord, for having given orders that I was to be well treated in your house and restored to health. It has been a very interesting experience for me."

"I can believe that!" the Marquis said. "Perhaps you have never slept under a roof before?"

Again she gave him that strange smile which made him feel as if he had said something rather ridiculous. But he told himself it was just a trick she had.

"Where have you come from?" he asked, "I mean, from what country?"

She hesitated and, before she could reply, the door opened and The Reverend came in.

"Ah, there you are, My Lord!" he exclaimed. "I heard you had arrived. It is a pleasure to welcome you back so soon, and I see you have made the acquaintance of my new pupil."

The Marquis shook hands with The Reverend and asked in surprise:

"Your new pupil?"

"Saviya has the most intelligent brain and the most remarkable memory I have ever encountered," The Reverend said enthusiastically.

The Marquis looked astonished.

"All in one small person?" he asked.

"You may not believe it, My Lord, but she absorbs a new subject in a manner which I consider phenomenal," The Reverend said, almost as if Saviya was not present.

She was listening, but still, the Marquis noted, with that faint smile on her lips.

"I had an idea," the Marquis said slowly, "although of course I must have been mistaken, that Gypsies could not read or write."

"That is true," Saviya agreed, "and they do not wish to do so. They memorise what they hear and there are story-tellers who translate our legends into poem or song. Besides, for a Gypsy who is always on the move, there is no room for books."

"And yet," the Marquis said, "from what I have just heard, you can read!"

"I am the exception!"

And then, still with that faint mocking smile on her lips, she added:

"But you see, I am a witch!"

"A witch?" the Marquis echoed in astonishment.

"But naturally!" she answered. "Otherwise I should not be able to qualify for the very flattering report the Reverend Gentleman has just given of me."

The Marquis was intrigued.

"You will both have to tell me much more about this," he said. "First of all I want to know where Saviya has come from, and why her tribe has visited Ruckley—it seems, for the first time."

"I have learnt, not from Saviya, but from other people in the neighbourhood," The Reverend answered, "that the Gypsies have certain places which they visit in rotation. Ruckley is one of them, as I told you, My Lord, by arrangement with your grandmother."

"I had not forgotten," the Marquis said briefly. "What interests me is that we should attract not only English Gypsies but foreign ones."

"All Gypsies are foreign," Saviya said. "We have no place that we can call our own."

"And why is that?"

"We are condemned to wander the earth," she answered, "perhaps for the expiation of past sins, perhaps because for us that is happiness."

The Marquis sat down on the edge of the desk.

"Will you please answer the question I have already asked you?" he said. "Where have you just come from?"

"Germany."

"And before that?"

"We came across Poland from Russia."

"Now let me think," the Marquis said. "I have a

feeling that the Russians treat their Gypsies in a different way from other countries. Is that true?"

"All countries at some time or other have persecuted the Gypsies," Saviya answered, "with the exception of the Russians. There we have a different status altogether."

"Why?" the Marquis enquired.

"Because of our music and because the Russians appreciate our dances."

The Marquis looked at her slight figure and realised that even standing still, she had a grace about her that he had not noticed in other women.

"You are a dancer?" he asked.

She nodded her head.

"I have been taught by my mother, who was the daughter of one of the greatest of all Gypsy dancers in Russia. Grand Dukes and Princes fought with each other so that she should appear in their private theatres, and on several occasions she danced before the Tsar."

"It is fascinating, is it not?" The Reverend exclaimed. "These are the things I always wanted to hear, and never until now have I had the chance of learning anything about the Gypsy race."

"Tell us more," the Marquis said to Saviya.

"So that you can laugh at us?" she enquired.

"You know I would not do that," he answered seriously. "I am as interested as The Reverend is, because we both realise how lamentably ignorant we are where your race is concerned."

"The Gypsies prefer people not to know about them," Saviya replied. "It is good that they should be mysterious, so that when they leave there is little to remember."

A footman came into the room to inform The Reverend that someone wanted to see him.

"Do not leave before I return, My Lord," he begged.

"I am in no hurry," the Marquis replied.

As the door shut behind him, the Marquis said to Saviya:

"Come, sit down and talk to me."

He walked to the window as he spoke where in the summer there were comfortable chairs arranged so that from the Library one could look out on the velvet green lawns which ended in a yew-hedge beyond which was the Herb-Garden.

The Marquis seated himself in an arm-chair and Saviya sat on the end of the window-seat, her face turned from the Marquis so that he could see the exquisite outline of her profile.

He tried to think of what she reminded him, but it was hard to say if there was a characteristic from any other race to be distinguished in her features.

'She is beautifull' he thought suddenly, and yet her beauty was neither classical nor did it belong to any one artistic period.

She was simply unique, with green eyes slanting up a little at the corners, an oval face which ended in a small pointed chin below lips which, when she smiled, curved in that strangely mocking manner.

Her hair hung as it had the first time the Marquis had seen her, straight down her back to below her waist, and now he saw that she wore earrings also made of coins to match her necklace, and they glittered in the sunshine as she moved her head.

"Has Hobley given you the money as I instructed him?" the Marquis asked suddenly.

Saviya turned her face from the window to look at him.

"I do not want your money," she answered.

As she spoke, the Marquis realised that the coins around her neck and in her ears were worth a hundred times more than the five pounds with which he had thought to recompense her for her injuries.

He also had an uneasy suspicion that the red stones he had supposed were glass were in fact rubies.

Then he told himself he must be in a state of stupidity. How could Gypsies be expected to own anything so valuable?

"Tell me about your tribe, the Kalderash," he said.

"I have told you that we are the metal-workers," Saviya answered in a tone that was almost reproving, because she must repeat herself.

"And what metals do you use?" the Marquis enquired.

"Copper, silver or gold. Whatever is necessary for the work we have to do," Saviya replied.

"Gold?" the Marquis questioned.

"The Nobles in Hungary use goblets for their wine and vessels of every description to ornament their tables. It is the Kalderash who fashion them."

"You liked being in Hungary?" the Marquis said, and added before she could answer:

"I have the feeling the Hungarians call you something rather special."

"In Hungary and in Germany our Chiefs are 'the Dukes of Little Egypt.' "

"An important designation! Does it please you?"

"Sometimes we are Kings, in Germany the 'Zigeuner,' in France 'Bohemians,' in Turkey the 'Tchinghanie,' and in Persia 'Karaki.' What does it matter? We are still Gypsies."

"But more appreciated in some countries than in others."

"King Sigismund of Hungary gave the Gypsies letters of protection. James V of Scotland gave one of our patrons, Johnie Faur, Lord and Earl of Little Egypt, juridical rights over his own Gypsy Bands."

"How do you know that?" the Marquis asked.

"Our history is passed by mouth from tribe to tribe so that we know where we may find friends," Saviya answered.

"That is good sense," the Marquis said. "I would very much like to meet the rest of your tribe. May I come to your camp?"

"No!"

The refusal was positive.

"Why not?"

"Because if they see you, I shall not be able to come here again."

The Marquis was surprised.

"But why?"

"You would not understand."

"What would I not understand?"

Saviya hesitated before she said:

"My Father, who is the Chief of the Kalderash, or, as we call him, the 'Voivode,' allowed me to come here and read your books because you were not at home. If he knows that you are back, then I cannot come again."

"But what has your father got against me?" the Marquis asked incredulously.

"You are a man!"

"Explain what you are trying to say," he begged.

"Perhaps another time," Saviya said, rising to her feet. "It is getting late. I must return or they will come in search of me."

"Return where?" the Marquis asked.

"To where we are camped in your woods."

"But I thought you were staying here in the House!"

"Only for the first two days when I was unconscious," Saviya replied. "But because Mr. Hobley was so kind and treated my wounds, I was allowed to return to have them dressed. Then, because I begged and besought my Father to let me read some of your books, he agreed. But there must be no other reason for me to visit your house."

"But you will come tomorrow?" the Marquis asked.

"I think it will be permitted."

"Then do not tell your father that I am here."

She gave him a glance from under her long lashes.

"Please come tomorrow," the Marquis begged. "There is so much I want to learn about you. Why you are a witch, for instance, and what strange enchantments you can perform."

Saviya smiled but did not answer.

Instead she moved away from the Marquis and, as she crossed the floor of the Library, he thought he had never seen a woman move with such grace—she seemed to float rather than walk.

As she reached the door she looked back at him.

"You will come tomorrow?" the Marquis insisted.

"If it is possible," she replied.

Then she was gone.

The Marquis stood quite still for a moment staring at the closed door.

"A witch!" he said aloud. "That is certainly a being I never expected to encounter!"

Chapter Three

The Marquis rose early the following morning, as he realised he must go over to Eurydice's house and arrange about taking over the management of her Estate.

As Hobley helped him put on riding-clothes, he said: "You did a good job on our Gypsy, Hobley."

"The wound healed quickly because she was so healthy," Hobley replied, "and it was in fact, M'Lord, a pleasure."

The Marquis raised his eyebrows and asked:

"Did the rest of the household get over their fears of what she might do to them?"

"Yes indeed, M'Lord," Hobley answered. "She captivated all of them before she finished. Even Mrs. Meedham spoke well of the young lady!"

The Marquis was amused to notice that Saviya had changed from being "one of them gypsies" to a "young lady," and he realised it was indeed a compliment.

There was no-one more snobbish or more rigid in their sense of propriety than the servants in a Nobleman's house.

The slightest infringement of their privileges or of their recognised order of precedence would cause almost a revolution in their ranks.

That they were no longer frightened of Saviya but had accepted her was, the Marquis thought, a very unusual and unpredictable change in their attitude.

51

He did not, however, express his thoughts to Hobley but merely remarked:

"The Reverend seems to think very highly of her intelligence."

"The Reverend is a good judge of character, M'Lord," Hobley said stoutly.

The Marquis found himself thinking of Saviya as he rode across the Park and then through the woods towards Eurydice's house.

Trees covered many acres of land in that part of Hertfordshire, and as the Marquis moved through them he realised that it would be easy for not one band of Gypsies but dozens to hide themselves away so that it would be difficult for anyone to find them.

He, however, had a vague idea as to where they would be camping, and he thought that when he had the time he would perhaps visit them unexpectedly and see what they were like.

At the same time, if Saviya was to be believed, that would mean her visits to the House would be stopped. At the moment that was something which he had no wish to happen.

He wondered if she was speaking the truth.

He had always believed Gypsies were free and easy, and the women dispensed their favours to whomever they fancied.

If they did, the Marquis thought with a faint smile, they would be behaving just like the more aristocratic members of their sex in the *Beau Monde*.

There was no doubt that sexual morality in the Social World was very lax.

The raffish Society which was centred round Carlton House had since the very beginning of the century, set an example that was, to say the least, regrettable, while London itself was, as the Marquis well knew, a hot-bed of vice.

A man would have had to be blind not to notice the ever-increasing numbers of painted wantons who haunted the streets at night.

Some of them were but children, and the Flash

Houses, where boys were taught to steal, pick pockets and commit every other minor crime in the calendar, grew more uncontrollable every year.

There were so many evils that should be denounced and reformed, the Marquis thought, and wondered if he himself should speak on the subject when the opportunity arose in the House of Lords.

Then, he thought with a wry smile, he was hardly the person to take a stand against immorality or to constitute himself a champion of good morals.

He could see the faces of many alluring women looking at him with a fire burning in their eyes, their white arms reaching out, their lips surrendering themselves with an ease which told him without words he was by no means their first lover—nor would he be their last.

And yet he was prepared to bet quite a considerable sum that the Gypsy girl he had knocked down with his Phaeton was intrinsically pure.

At the thought he laughed aloud.

'Really, I must be besotted to imagine such a thing is possible,' he told himself.

After all, Saviya admitted, if she was to be believed, to having visited Russia, Hungary, and Germany. To reach these countries she must have passed through many others. Was it likely that on her travels she had not with her strange beauty aroused attention?

And what about the men of her own tribe? They would have eyes in their heads and warm blood in their veins!

The Marquis emerged from the woods to see in front of him Eurydice's house, and at the sight of it he deliberately put the thoughts of Saviya and all the other women he had known out of his mind.

He was certain that ahead of him lay a great deal of hard thinking and perhaps quite a considerable amount of work.

He was not mistaken.

When he arrived home at luncheon time, he knew

53

that there was no chance of his returning to London for at least a week.

He was in fact appalled at the mess in which Eurydice had left her properties.

Her instructions were very clear.

They were to be handed over to his administration, and all future orders and of course the payment of employees was to come from Ruckley.

Anyone else, the Marquis thought, might have resented having such a problem—and an expensive one —thrust upon him without notice, but he guessed that Eurydice had known that her decision was in a way his triumph.

His father had always wished to acquire the neighbouring land and make it a part of the Ruckley Estate. Now, to all intents and purposes, this had happened!

The Marquis interviewed the Agent, the Farm-Managers and Eurydice's Attorney, who was waiting with a number of papers which required his signature.

As he rode home, the Marquis told himself that it was essential that he should give the new land his personal and immediate attention in order to rectify the loss of revenue he had discovered.

He was still debating who he would put in charge and how to dove-tail the management of the two Estates when he reached home.

It needed a quarter of an hour to luncheon time, and the Marquis handed his hat and riding-whip to a footman and walked automatically towards the Library.

As he expected, The Reverend was there and so was Saviya.

They were so interested in what they were reading that the Marquis was half-way across the room before they noticed him.

Then they turned round and there was no mistaking the expression of gladness in their eyes at the sight of him.

"Here you are, My Lord!" The Reverend exclaimed. "You left very early this morning, before I had time to tell you of my new discovery."

"Good-morning, Sir," the Marquis said, "and good-morning to you, Saviya."

She smiled at him, and he thought how lovely she looked: her hair very dark against the brilliant bindings of the books; the movement of her hands even more graceful than he had remembered.

"Good-morning, My Lord."

Then, like a child that has something exciting to relate, she added:

"The Reverend Gentleman has found a book which he is sure will please you."

"What is it?" the Marquis enquired.

"It is a book on Gypsies by one John Howland," The Reverend replied, holding it out to the Marquis. "I had no idea it was in the Library, but actually it was only published two years ago in 1816. It relates all you wished to know about the origin of the Gypsies."

The Marquis took the book from him.

"I suppose my father must have bought it."

"That is so, and because he died that same year it must have been overlooked," The Reverend replied, "which was why I had not included it in the Catalogue."

The Marquis opened the book, turned the pages and remarked:

"I see it has a comparative list of the Gypsy and Hindustani language. Some of the words seem very similar."

"That is true," Saviya said. "For instance I would describe you in English as a very important man, or Prince. The word is Rajah in Hindustani and Raja in Romany."

"I shall have to study this," the Marquis said, "but at the moment I am extremely hungry and also thirsty. Will you join me in a glass of wine, Reverend?"

"I shall be delighted, My Lord."

"And I hope, Saviya," the Marquis said, "that you will have luncheon with me."

She hesitated for a moment, then answered:

"I would like that."

"It is no use my inviting you, Reverend, is it?" the Marquis asked.

The elderly man shook his head.

"You know with my poor digestion I can eat only once a day."

"I had not really forgotten," the Marquis replied.

They went into the Salon, and after The Reverend had accepted a small glass of Madeira, he returned to the Library.

Saviya looked at the Marquis's shining riding-boots and said:

"You have been riding. I have admired the magnificent horses in your stables."

"I imagine that you ride?"

She smiled and answered:

"It is something I enjoy doing more than anything else except dancing."

"I hope to see you do both."

They went into luncheon and the Marquis wondered how she would eat. Surely, he thought, a Gypsy would not know either the etiquette or the proper behaviour expected at a Gentleman's table.

But it would have been impossible, he realised, for Saviya to do anything that was not graceful or elegant. He noticed, however, that she did not pick up a knife or fork until she could follow him.

Yet it was cleverly done and anyone who had not been observing her closely would not have noticed that she was imitating not only his choice of cutlery but also the manner in which he used it.

But after a time the Marquis forgot to watch Saviya for any faults she might commit. He was too much interested in what she was saying to think of anything else.

He had little difficulty in persuading her to talk of her travels.

The Marquis was an expert at drawing a woman out, obtaining her confidence and making her feel so secure and happy in his company that she could trust him with her innermost secrets.

Usually he did not exert himself unduly in this way, but he knew without consciously thinking of it that he had the power at his command.

Because he was quite certain that Saviya had never had luncheon alone with a man before, and certainly not in such agreeable circumstances, it was easy to make her talk.

She told him of how the Gypsies trekked across Europe, moving from country to country, often having to flee from cruel persecutions by the Authorities, but usually welcomed by the ordinary people, because of their special crafts, sorcery and horse-dealing.

"My father is a great authority on horse-flesh," Saviya said, "and he has often been commissioned to buy animals in one country and send them to another."

"How big is your tribe?" the Marquis asked.

"When we left Hungary for Russia, there were two hundred of us," Saviya replied, "but usually we number but forty to fifty as we are here in England."

"Do you sleep in tents?"

"We used to," she answered, "but now we have something new."

"What is that?"

"We have acquired caravans. There are not many in England yet, but in Europe a number of Gypsies have them. Caravans have always been used by the Circus people, but they are so attractive and comfortable that now all the Gypsies that can afford it wish to own one."

When luncheon was over the Marquis and Saviya went to the stables and he at once realised, as he might have expected, that she had a special way with horses.

"What magic do you use on a restless or savage horse?" he asked, when she had entered the stable of a stallion of whom even the Marquis's grooms were wary.

"It is a secret which belongs only to the Gypsies," Saviya answered, "and must certainly not be imparted to a Gorgio."

"Is that what I am?" the Marquis asked.

"Anyone who is not a Gypsy is a Gorgio or Gadje," she replied.

"And what do you call yourselves?"

"We are the Rom," Saviya replied proudly.

When they had finished inspecting the stables, the Marquis took Saviya round the old part of the House, showing her the Priests' holes, where the Catholic Priests had hidden from Queen Elizabeth's soldiers, who would have burned them at the stake.

The hiding-places had been used later in the history of the Ruckleys, when Cromwell had defeated the Royalists and hung many of them on Tyburn Hill.

As the Marquis showed Saviya round his home, he found himself recalling family stories and legends that he had known as a boy.

He liked the concentrated attention she gave to everything he said: the light in her eyes; the way her lips curved differently from the mysterious mocking smile she had given him yesterday.

Finally, they reached the end of the long Picture Gallery where he had shown her paintings of his ancestors, and the Marquis stood at the casement window looking out into the garden.

There was a fountain just below them where a stone cupid held a huge fish in his hands. From its mouth a jet of water spouted high, which glittered iridescent in the sunshine.

"You are very lucky," Saviya said in a low voice.

"Am I?" the Marquis asked.

"You do not always think so," she said, "but one day you will realise how important this House and everything it contains is to your happiness."

"I think I realise it now," the Marquis said. "Are you telling my fortune, Saviya?"

"No, not really," she answered, "but at the same time there is something I do not like."

It seemed to the Marquis that her voice had changed.

Now she turned her head to look at him and he had the strange feeling she was not actually seeing him but looking through and beyond him.

"Yes, there is danger," she said in a low tone. "You must be careful! You have an enemy. It is a man and he is trying to injure you."

"How do you know that?" the Marquis asked sharply. "Has Hobley been talking to you?"

"I know it because he is there," Saviya answered. "I can see him quite clearly. He is dark, he has a long nose, and his name has the same first letter as yours. You must be careful . . . very careful where he is concerned!"

"How do you know this?" the Marquis asked again.

As he spoke, his voice almost harsh, Saviya shook her head as if she would dispel something that was hurting her and from which she would be free.

Then she knelt on the window-seat and looked out into the garden.

The Marquis did not speak for a moment and then he said:

"What you have told me is true, but I cannot understand how you can be aware of something which concerns only my private life."

"I told you I am a witch."

"I thought you were joking."

"Magic is not a joke to the Kalderash. It is a part of us and part of our destiny; we cannot escape it."

"What you have told me is true," the Marquis repeated, "but you did not say if my enemy would be successful in what he is attempting to do to me."

There was a silence, and then Saviya, still not looking at him, said:

"I have warned you of danger. That is enough. A man prepared is already armed."

"I hope you are right!"

She turned her face suddenly.

"Be careful! Please be very careful!" she pleaded.

Her eyes met his and for a moment it seemed as if something passed between them and it was impossible for either of them to move.

Almost without meaning to, the Marquis put out his arms towards Saviya.

It was an instinctive gesture—something he had done so often in his life, when he had been attracted by a lovely woman, that he did not even consider what her reaction would be.

He just followed his impulse.

Then as his hands touched her, as he would have drawn her close against him—and had already bent his lips towards hers, she gave a little twist of her body.

She was free of him, and he saw incredulously that she held in her hand a long, shining dagger—a stiletto such as the Italians carried.

She held it firmly in her hand between her breasts, the sharp point directed at his chest.

Slowly the Marquis dropped his arms.

For a moment neither of them spoke, and then Saviya said:

"You are a Gorgio. You must not touch me. It is forbidden."

"Why?"

"No Rom can associate with a Gorgio. If she does she is exiled from the tribe."

"Do you really mean that?" the Marquis asked in genuine surprise. "Tell me about it, Saviya, and put away that dangerous weapon. I promise I will not touch you without your permission."

She looked at him searchingly, as if not sure whether she should trust him. Then so swiftly that he hardly saw it happen, the stiletto disappeared into her bodice and she sat down on the window seat.

"I am very ignorant of your rules," the Marquis said, "so you must please forgive me if I offended you."

He spoke beguilingly and a very much more experienced woman than Saviya would have found it hard to resist him.

"If you had been here with a . . . lady of your own race," she asked hesitatingly, "would you have . . . kissed her?"

"I have a feeling," the Marquis said, "that she would have been very disappointed if I had not attempted to do so."

He smiled as he spoke, but Saviya's face was serious.

"If she had been unmarried, would you not have felt obliged to ask her to be your . . . wife?"

"If she were unmarried," the Marquis answered, "it is most unlikely that we should be here together unchaperoned."

"And had she been married?"

"Then in most cases the lady in question would have expected me to show my admiration for her charms."

"If she had been a Gypsy, her husband would have beaten her for such behaviour," Saviya said sternly, "and in France her head would have been shaved."

"Shaved!" the Marquis ejaculated. "Is that really true?"

"It is a common punishment among Gypsies," Saviya answered, "and for many months a woman who has aroused her husband's jealousy becomes an object of shame in the eyes of the tribe."

"Then Gypsy husbands beat their wives!" the Marquis said.

"There are worse punishments if they behave improperly," Saviya told him. "But it does not happen often. Gypsy marriages are very happy and they last forever!"

"Even if they do not get on together?" the Marquis enquired.

"We are a happy people," Saviya answered. "Family life is sacred and anyone who offends against the sanctity of their marriage deserves the punishment they receive."

She spoke with some conviction, and the Marquis knew that what she was saying must be the truth. Nevertheless he was astonished.

"Who will you marry, Saviya?" he asked.

"I shall not know that until he approaches my father."

"You have no choice?"

"In the Kalderash a marriage is always arranged between the fathers of the bride and bride-groom. A betrothed girl has no right either to visit or to talk to the man she will marry, even when other people are present."

"Surely that is very strange?" the Marquis said.

"I think perhaps it is something we have inherited from our Indian ancestors," Saviya replied. "Whatever the origin of the custom, a gold coin is placed on the girl's neck and this marks her as *Tomnimi*—promised."

"What happens," the Marquis enquired, "if a Gypsy man or woman falls in love with a Gorgio?"

"In either case it brings exclusion and exile from the tribe," Saviya said.

"For life?" the Marquis enquired.

"The woman or the man, is held in contempt, indeed hated, and no-one will speak to the offender. They are *Poshrats, Didikais,* they no longer exist."

"It is a very harsh code!"

Then the Marquis asked:

"Does not the idea of marrying someone you have never seen, whom you do not know and whom you may not even like, frighten you?"

Saviya looked away, and he had the feeling that he had touched on some secret that she had kept hidden, perhaps even from herself.

She did not reply and after a moment he said in his deep voice:

"Tell me. I want to know, Saviya."

"Yes," she said hesitatingly, "the idea does . . . frighten me."

"Do you not think," the Marquis asked, "that love is more important than anything else? Is there no place for love among the Gypsies?"

"A woman should love her husband," Saviya answered.

"And if she finds it impossible?" the Marquis insisted. "If for instance she falls in love with another man before marriage, would that not seem to her more important than tribal laws and regulations?"

"I do not know," Saviya replied, "it has never happened to me."

"And yet you have thought about it," the Marquis persisted. "Perhaps too, Saviya, you have dreamt of a man that you could love, a man who could capture your heart and make it his."

His voice was very deep and now, as she turned her eyes to look at him, he thought there was an expression in them like that of a very small and frightened animal.

Then she said after a moment:

"But the laws of the Kalderash are just and my people believe in them."

"But you—you are different," the Marquis said. "You are a witch and so perhaps more sensitive and capable of deeper feelings than the others."

"Why do you say such things to me?"

"Because you are so beautiful," the Marquis replied. "Because you are not only unbelievably lovely, but because you have a brain. It is the intelligent people in this world who suffer the most, Saviya."

She did not answer, but he saw a little quiver run through her.

"It is the difference between a race-horse and an animal that draws a cart," he went on. "You know as well as I do that the one is far more highly strung, far more sensitive to pain than the other."

Saviya was silent and then she said:

"It is best not to think of . . . love."

"But you do think of it," the Marquis replied. "And something that you cannot control yearns for it."

His words seemed to vibrate between them. Then, as he waited for her answer, there was the sound of footsteps at the far end of the Picture Gallery and a familiar voice cried:

"Ah, here you are, Fabius! I was told you were going round the House."

The Marquis turned his head to see Charles Collington advancing toward him.

"I received your note," the Captain said as he walked over the shining oak floor. "I felt there must be some very unusual reason for you to stay in the country, so I have ridden to the rescue, if that is the right word!"

"I was merely informing you that I could not dine with you tonight," the Marquis said.

"Nevertheless I felt it was important for me to be with you," Charles Collington replied.

He reached the Marquis's side to stand with a look of surprise on his face, staring at Saviya.

"Let me introduce you," the Marquis said. "Captain Charles Collington—Saviya, a very lovely Gypsy whom I ran over with my Phaeton."

"That was an original way of getting yourself introduced!" Charles Collington exclaimed.

He put out his hand to Saviya and went on:

"It is delightful to meet you, Miss Saviya."

She dropped him a small curtsy.

"I must go now," she said to the Marquis.

"No, please do not leave us," the Marquis begged. "This is my great friend, and I know when I tell him about you, he will not believe a word I say unless you assure him that I am speaking the truth."

"Did His Lordship say that you were a Gypsy?" Charles Collington asked Saviya with undisguised interest.

"She is indeed!" the Marquis answered, "and she has opened my eyes to a whole new world I did not know existed."

"I have always been a great admirer of the Gypsies," Charles Collington said. "When we were fighting in Portugal, the Ciganos, as they were called,
were extremely useful. They could move between the
two Armies without fear. They were neither friend
nor foe, and in consequence they carried messages and
spied for both sides!"

"Now that I think about it, I believe you are right!"
the Marquis said. "I never paid much attention to the
Portuguese Gypsies myself."

"Gypsies do not wish you to pay them attention,"
Saviya said with a smile. "What they would like most
would be to be invisible. To come and go with no-one
troubling about them."

"Well, I am very glad that you are not invisible!"
Charles Collington said with a look of frank admiration in his eyes. "No wonder His Lordship is in no
hurry to return to London. Having seen you, I find it
a most compelling reason for preferring the country!"

"I expect you would like a drink, if you have ridden
here from London," the Marquis interposed. "How
long did it take you?"

"An hour and thirty-five minutes," Charles Collington replied. "It is not a record, but I did not hurry
myself. My horses are not as good as yours, Fabius."

"It usually takes me an hour and fifteen minutes,"
the Marquis said. "That is, across country. It takes
longer by road."

"I do not mind how long it has taken. I am delighted to be here," Charles Collington said, his eyes
on Saviya.

The Marquis noticed that she drew a little away
from him, as if she felt he was encroaching upon her.

When they went downstairs for Charles Collington
to have a glass of wine after his ride, it was to find tea
had been laid in the Salon.

They sampled a few of the vast selection of sandwiches, cakes and small delicacies for which the Chef
at Ruckley House was famous.

As they ate and Charles Collington described in

graphic detail a Ball he had attended the night before, he said to the Marquis:

"By the way, Sir Algernon was there and sneering because none of us had yet attempted to win his wager of the thousand guineas."

"A thousand guineas for a wager?" Saviya exclaimed. "What a huge sum!"

"It is nothing compared to what some fools lose gaming," Charles Collington replied. "Over twenty thousand pounds changed hands last night at White's alone. Needless to say, none of it came my way!"

"You are poor?" Saviya asked sympathetically.

"Absolutely starving!" Charles Collington replied.

The Marquis laughed.

"Do not believe him, Saviya. He is quite warm in the pocket, but he is extravagant, like all the gay young men who frequent the gambling Clubs of St. James's."

"Gypsies like to gamble," Saviya said, "but it is usually on cock-fights or sport of some sort."

"And very much more sensible," Charles Collington approved. "When you come to think of it, it is exceedingly silly to throw away money on the turn of a card. No-one ever ends up a winner."

"That is true," the Marquis agreed.

"All the same," Charles Collington said, "I should like to confound Sir Algernon with his own words. He is so certain that he is infallible that it irritates me."

He paused before he said slowly:

"Do you suppose that Gibbon would ever think that Miss Saviya was a Gypsy?"

"It is something I am sure I would never have thought of myself," the Marquis said, "except for the fact that she was dressed like one."

"If she were gowned like a Lady of Quality," Charles Collington cried, "I am convinced that Gibbon would never suspect for a moment that she was anything else."

"It is certainly an idea," the Marquis replied.

"What are you talking about?" Saviya enquired in a bewildered voice.

They told her the details of Sir Algernon's bet and she laughed.

"He must be very sure that you have no chance of winning, for him to wager so much money!"

"He is too sure!" Captain Collington said. "That is why we have to show him up for the pompous snob he is! The whole contention is baloney, if you ask me! Everyone's blood is red if you prick them!"

"Or knock them down with a Phaeton," the Marquis said, looking at the mark on Saviya's forehead.

"Now do take this seriously, Fabius," Charles Collington said. "We have found the ideal person to confound Gibbon and make him eat his words."

"It might succeed," the Marquis said, "but one of the difficulties would be how to persuade Gibbon to come down here and meet Saviya. I have a feeling she would not be allowed to come to London with us."

"I am quite certain my father would say no," Saviya agreed.

"Then somehow we have to inveigle Sir Algernon to Ruckley without his becoming suspicious," the Marquis said.

"That is a real problem," Charles Collington said reflectively. "What are his interests?"

"Shooting, for one thing," the Marquis said. "He has shot here in the past, but it is not the time of year for pheasant or partridge."

"No, of course not," Charles agreed. "What else?"

"I have it!" the Marquis exclaimed.

His friend waited expectantly and he went on:

"The one thing Sir Algernon really cares about, besides his Family Tree, is his collection of ancient coins."

"Something I have always found extremely boring," Charles Collington said. "So where does that get us?"

"Quite a long way," the Marquis replied.

As he spoke he looked at the necklace of coins around Saviya's neck.

"Tell me," he said, "has your tribe any loose coins that we could borrow for a day. I see that some of those you wear round your neck are Roman. Have you any more?"

"A large number," Saviya replied.

"If we could tell Sir Algernon that we have found half a dozen coins in one of the fields," the Marquis went on, "and we want advice as to whether we should dig for more, I am certain he would be extremely intrigued."

"That is brilliant!" Charles Collington exclaimed. "Sit down and write a letter now and I will carry it back to London with me."

"I will send a groom," the Marquis said. "He might be suspicious if you were my messenger. He might guess we were collaborating."

"Which we undoubtedly are!" Charles Collington said. "But do not forget we have to find a suitable gown for Saviya, decide who she is to be, and where she comes from."

"The whole thing will be quite a Drury Lane production by the time we have finished," the Marquis laughed.

"Why not?" Charles Collington answered. "A thousand guineas is a thousand guineas."

"May I remind you," the Marquis remarked, "that we have not yet obtained Saviya's agreement to assist us in the masquerade?"

"I feel that I might let you down," Saviya said in a soft voice. "I am a Gypsy, and it is very unlikely that anyone would take me for an English Lady of Quality."

"Who said anything about your being English?" the Marquis asked. "That would be ridiculous."

"You mean . . . I do not sound like an English woman?"

"I hope you will not be disappointed," the Marquis replied, "but you have an unmistakable foreign accent. It is very attractive—in fact it is enchanting—but it is definitely foreign!"

"It is because I have been in England for only a short time," Saviya said. "When we have lived in a country for six months or a year, everyone tells me I speak their language perfectly."

"The phenomenal memory of which The Reverend spoke," the Marquis smiled.

"Then she must be a foreigner," Charles Collington said. "It does not matter—and we can give her a high-sounding name and title. In fact it will make it even more difficult for Sir Algernon to suspect that she is not who she pretends to be."

"Which country do you fancy, Saviya?" the Marquis asked.

She thought for a moment.

"My mother was Russian and I have lived in St. Petersburg and Moscow for nearly ten years of my life. It is obvious that I should be Russian."

"You are right!" Charles Collington cried. "And you look mysterious and excitingly Russian with that black hair and that ivory skin!"

There was a flirtatious note in Charles Collington's voice which the Marquis did not miss.

"I think perhaps you should go now, Saviya," he said. "I would not wish your father to be incensed because you are late, and it is important that you should not be forbidden to return to the house. Will you enquire if we may borrow the coins?"

"I will bring them tomorrow," Saviya replied.

She made a deep curtsy to the Marquis and a very brief one to Charles Collington. Then she moved away from them down the Long Gallery, and they both of them watched her graceful figure until she disappeared through the doorway at the far end.

Charles Collington gave an exclamation.

"My God, Fabius," he said, "you are a dark horse! Where did you find anything so entrancing, so fascinating, so incredibly beautiful?"

Chapter Four

The Marquis, dressing for dinner, thought with satisfaction that so far everything had gone well.

Sir Algernon Gibbon had arrived early in the afternoon, and the Marquis and Charles Collington had taken him out to a newly-ploughed field to show him where they said they had found seven Roman coins.

He had become extremely excited, saying that they were not only of great antiquity but in his opinion very valuable, and he strongly advised the Marquis to dig deeper in the immediate neighbourhood of the find in case there were other treasures as yet undiscovered.

He went into a long dissertation on the way the Romans built their Amphitheatres and the construction of their villas, and pointed out with reason that there were many Roman remains at the neighbouring town of St. Albans.

The Marquis had listened with flattering attention, being more punctilious in this particular than he would have been otherwise, because he knew that Charles Collington was restless.

What occupied his friend's mind were the plans they had made for the evening. The Marquis thought with a smile that no-one could have taken more trouble to ensure that their campaign to deceive Sir Algernon was mapped out down to the last detail.

He also told himself that never had he spent a

more amusing time than he had the last few days, when they had been teaching Saviya her part.

She had been, as the Marquis expected, a quick-brained and tremendously receptive pupil.

They only had to tell her something once: never did she forget or fail to carry out their instructions to perfection.

What had pleased the Marquis was that, while Charles Collington had taken upon himself the role of producer, it was to himself that Saviya regularly looked not only for confirmation of what was said but for approval when she did what was asked of her.

He found himself waiting for that half-shy and yet trusting little glance she gave him.

It was as if she realised that he was a greater authority than Charles Collington and, what was more, she valued his opinion more than anyone else's.

Charles Collington could not praise her enough!

"She is fantastic!" he kept saying over and over again. "No-one would believe she was a Gypsy or that she had not been born into one of the highest families in the land! She is a living example of our contention that it is not blue blood which makes a lady, but education."

"And sensitivity," the Marquis added.

"Of course," his friend replied, "Saviya is unusually sensitive and receptive to everything one says or does."

"You are a born actress," the Marquis said to her once and she replied:

"I think that good acting depends on experiencing one's rôle emotionally as well as mentally. A dancer has to feel deeply everything she portrays, so perhaps it is not as difficult for me as for other people."

It was this remark which had given the Marquis an idea for another way in which they could confound Sir Algernon Gibbon, and this was something which concerned Saviya and him more than Charles Collington.

What made everything so much easier—Saviya told them with a note of surprise in her voice—was that her father had withdrawn his objection to her coming to the house even though he knew the Marquis was in residence.

What was more he approved of their plan that Saviya should act the part of a Russian Noblewoman.

"Why has your father changed his mind about me?" the Marquis enquired.

"I do not know," Saviya answered. "I expected he would be angry and forbid me to take part in your Masquerade, but he was amused by it and only admonished me to act so well that you would win your wager."

She paused and then she added:

"I think perhaps he feels it is the same as performing in the private theatres in Moscow and St. Petersburg."

"You have done that?" the Marquis asked.

"Only in a very small way," Saviya answered. "Amongst the Gypsies who live in both those cities there are many very famous dancers and prima donnas, and because I was my mother's daughter, I was occasionally allowed to take part, not particularly through my own merits."

"I want you to tell me about it," the Marquis said.

But they had been so busy preparing for Sir Algernon Gibbon's arrival that there had been no time to continue the conversation.

Now Hobley finished tying the Marquis's white cravat and, stepping back to look at his handiwork, he said:

"I think I ought to tell you, M'Lord, that Mr. Jethro has been in the village."

"When?" the Marquis asked sharply.

"He was there yesterday, M'Lord," Hobley replied. "I understand from one of the footmen who went to the post office this morning before luncheon that his curricle was outside The Green Man."

73

"What is he doing in the village, Hobley?" the Marquis enquired.

"I can't understand it, M'Lord. I should have thought that if Mr. Jethro was in the vicinity he would have called upon Your Lordship, but I understand he was making enquiries."

"About what?" the Marquis asked.

"Your Lordship's prolonged stay in the country, and also about Miss Saviya."

"Why should that interest him?" the Marquis asked almost to himself.

Then as Hobley did not reply he asked:

"How did you learn this?"

"Henry—he's the third footman, M'Lord—was in The Green Man yesterday when Mr. Jethro came in. He had two men with him, rather rough types, Henry thought."

"And he listened to their conversation?"

"It was not hard for him to do so, M'Lord. I understand Mr. Jethro was talking to the Landlord about Your Lordship, and then this morning he was in conversation with Bob."

"And who is Bob?" the Marquis asked.

"The new Pantry-Boy," Hobley replied. "Mr. Bush had difficulty in finding one and he took on this boy who said he came from St. Albans. I've discussed it with Mr. Bush, M'Lord, and we thought, in the circumstances, it would be best if we dispensed with Bob's services."

"You think," the Marquis said slowly, "that he is relaying information about the household to Mr. Jethro?"

"I should not be surprised, M'Lord. There was talk of money changing hands."

"Then dismiss him at once!" the Marquis said sharply. "I will not, as you well know, have any of my staff accepting bribes."

"We can't be sure, M'Lord," Hobley said, "that Bob knew Mr. Jethro before they got into conversation in

The Green Man, but Mr. Bush did mention that the reference Bob brought with him was from Lord Portgate, who Your Lordship well knows is a close friend of Mr. Jethro."

The Marquis recalled a dissolute, drunken young peer who was frequently in his cousin's company.

"Dismiss the boy!" the Marquis said briefly and, having been helped into his perfectly fitting evening coat, he went downstairs to the Salon.

There were only three for dinner—Sir Algernon Gibbon, Charles Collington and the Marquis.

The Chef had excelled himself, and the wine served with every course was superlative. The Gentlemen lingered over their Port in the Dining-Room for awhile and then repaired to the Salon.

They had not been there long before Bush came across the room to say in a low voice to the Marquis:

"There has been a slight accident to a lady's coach, M'Lord. Apparently the leading horse broke its rein. The grooms say they can have it repaired within half of an hour. I thought Your Lordship should know that the lady is outside."

"Then of course she must not wait there," the Marquis said. "Invite her in, Bush."

"Very good, M'Lord."

As the Butler left the room the Marquis turned to his friends and remarked:

"It appears we have company. I wonder if it is anyone we know."

"It is extremely annoying when a leading horse breaks its rein and one cannot control it," Charles Collington said. "It happened once to me on the way back from Brighton. I damned nearly had an accident."

Before anyone could reply, the door opened and Bush said in an impressive tone:

"Her Highness, Princess Kotovski, M'Lord."

The three gentlemen looked round to see a very elegant figure enter the room.

The lady had obviously discarded her wraps and

was attired in a dazzling evening gown of emerald green silk ornamented with tulle, caught with satin bows.

The new tight waist had just been re-introduced into London and there was no doubt that as she advanced towards them down the Salon she had the most exquisite figure.

Her face was even more arresting. She had black hair, with blue lights in it in the very latest fashion on top of her head, and her lovely eyes seemed very large in her oval face.

There was a necklace of emeralds from the Ruckley collection round her neck, and the same stones glittered in her small ears and in a bracelet which was clasped over her long kid-gloves.

The Marquis advanced to greet her.

"May I welcome you, Highness, to my house? I am the Marquis of Ruckley and deeply regret that you should have had an accident on the high road."

"I was fortunate in that I was just passing your gates," the newcomer replied in a musical voice, with a fascinating foreign accent. "Your grooms have been most obliging, My Lord, and I am extremely grateful."

"I am delighted we can be of service," the Marquis replied. "You are in fact, Ma'am, relieving the monotony of a bachelor party. Allow me to introduce my freinds—Sir Algernon Gibbon and Captain Charles Collington."

The lady dropped two extremely graceful curtsies and, having been seated on the damask sofa in front of the fire, accepted a glass of wine.

The Marquis offered her dinner, but she declared that she had already dined before she left Brochet Hall where she had been staying.

"Is your Highness proceeding to London?" Sir Algernon enquired.

The Princess smiled at him.

"My husband has just been appointed to the Russian Embassy," she replied. "It will be my first visit

76

to your famous capital and I am looking forward to it enormously."

"We must make sure you enjoy yourself, Ma'am," Captain Collington said. "I am sure you will, as the parties at the Russian Embassy are the gayest and most amusing given by the whole Diplomatic Corps."

"That is true," Sir Algernon agreed, "but then no country in the world can entertain better or more lavishly than your countrymen, Ma'am."

"I am glad to hear you say that," the Princess replied.

"I remember when I was in Russia," Sir Algernon went on, "being astonished at the magnificence of their hospitality."

"You have been to Russia?" the Marquis exclaimed. "I had no idea of that."

"It was a long time ago," Sir Algernon replied. "In the last year of the last century. I was but twenty at the time and doing a grand tour of the countries in Europe which were not at war."

"And you enjoyed my country?" the Princess enquired.

"I have never forgotten the beauty of it, the charm of its people, and of course its incomparable dancers," Sir Algernon replied.

The Marquis saw Saviya's eyes light up and hoped in her enthusiasm she would not forget the part she had to play.

"You speak, I suppose, of the Imperial Ballet, Sir Algernon," she said.

"Not only was the Imperial Ballet a delight beyond words," Sir Algernon replied, "but I was also entranced by your Gypsy dancers. In fact my Host, Prince Paul Borokowski, with whom I stayed, married some years later a dancer of the Gypsy race."

"Surely that was very unusual?" the Marquis asked, remembering what Saviya had said to him about a Gypsy marrying a Gorgio.

"Not in Russia," Sir Algernon replied. "There the

77

Gypsy dancers and singers have a special position that is quite different from anywhere else in the world."

The Marquis looked incredulous and, turning to the Princess, Sir Algernon went on:

"You will bear me out, Ma'am, when I say there are some Gypsies who inhabit stately houses, go abroad in their elegant equipages, and are not at all inferior to Russians of the highest rank in appearance or in intellect."

"Yes, that is true," Saviya admitted.

"And you will also agree," Sir Algernon continued, "that it is due not only to their amazing and magnificent dancing, but to the power of song."

He saw both the Marquis and Captain Collington were listening and said:

"Did you not know, Ruckley, that some of the best singers in the world have come from the Russian Gypsies? They have been acknowledged not only by the public of their own country, but by the most fastidious of foreign critics."

"I must admit that such a phenomenon had escaped my notice," the Marquis replied.

"Did you never hear of Catalani?" Sir Algernon enquired. "She was an Italian—one of the greatest Operatic Sopranos the world has ever known. She was so enchanted by the voice of a Moscow Gypsy when she heard her sing, that she tore from her shoulders a cashmere shawl that had been given to her by the Pope as the 'best singer in the world.'

" 'It is no longer mine by right,' the Italian declared, wrapping her shawl round the Gypsy."

"I must thank you for the kind things you say about my country," the Princess said, as Sir Algernon paused for breath.

"It is because what I found in Russia was so unique, so unforgettable," Sir Algernon replied, "that I really believe that it altered my life."

He paused for effect and went on:

"I have ever since cultivated the Arts, but I can

never surpass or even equal the magnificent treasures to be found in your Palaces, in the homes of your Princes."

"You make me envious, Gibbon," the Marquis remarked.

"It is true," Sir Algernon said.

He then went into a long discourse about the pictures he had seen in Moscow and the wonderful collections of Objets d'Art to be found in the Palaces of St. Petersburg.

He appealed to Saviya for confirmation of all he contended, and was delighted when she flattered him for being so discerning and knowledgeable on such matters.

When finally Bush came to say that the rein had been repaired and the carriage was now ready to convey her Highness to London, the Princess rose with a murmur of regret.

"You have been so kind!" she said to the Marquis. "What appeared at first to be a disaster has been changed into a delight!"

"I hope you will allow me to call on you as soon as I return to London," the Marquis replied.

"My husband and I will be delighted," the Princess answered, "and I know he will want to add his thanks to mine for your hospitality."

"We shall meet in the very near future," Sir Algernon said as she held out her hand to him. "The Russian Ambassador and his wife, Princess Lieven, are great friends of mine, and you must permit me to give a dinner-party in your honour as soon as you have had time to settle down."

"You are more than kind," the Princess said softly, and held out her hand to Captain Collington.

The Marquis escorted the Princess from the room and out into the Hall.

"You were magnificent!" he whispered, as soon as the door shut behind them. "How long do you want before I take Sir Algernon onto the terrace?"

"A quarter of an hour," she whispered.

Then the Marquis left her and went back into the Salon.

"What a beautiful woman!" Sir Algernon was exclaiming as he entered, "but then the Russians when they are young are unbelievably lovely. I am telling you the truth when I say there are no more beautiful women in the world than those of noble blood."

"I was interested in what you were saying about the Gypsies," Charles Collington remarked casually. "I have always thought of Gypsies as poor, ragged creatures wandering barefoot along the roads and sleeping under hedgerows or in tattered tents."

"Russian Gypsies are different," Sir Algernon replied. "Some of them are, of course, under the protection of the Grand Dukes and Princes."

"I always understood that Gypsies are very moral," the Marquis protested.

"They are never promiscuous," Sir Algernon replied. "My friend, Prince Paul explained to me that no real Gypsy ever becomes a prostitute. If they accept the protection of a Nobleman the liaison lasts for many years. The women in fact look on it as much the same as a marriage."

"And yet, you say some important Russians actually do marry Gypsies?" Charles Collington questioned incredulously.

"Many famous Gypsy singers and ballerinas have become Princesses," Sir Algernon answered. "He told me that it is not the aristocracy that objects to such a mésalliance but the Gypsies themselves who disapprove. They are a strange people who have no wish to intermix with other races."

The Marquis made sure that his guests' glasses were well-filled and then said:

"As it is a warm night, in fact surprisingly warm for the time of the year, I want you to come out onto the terrace. I have something to show you, Gibbon, which I think you will find unusual and very interesting."

"My visit to you has already been full of surprises,"

Sir Algernon replied. "I am therefore quite prepared for another."

The gentlemen walked out through the long French-windows which opened onto a flagged terrace. In the centre of it there was a flight of stone steps leading down to the lawn.

At the top of those were three arm-chairs.

The Marquis invited Sir Algernon to sit down in the centre while he and Charles Collington took a chair on either side of him.

The garden was quiet and mysterious under a star-strewn sky with a full moon just climbing up the Heavens.

In front of them the green lawn swept away to where there was a small Grecian Temple which had been brought to England by the Marquis's grand-father at the beginning of the eighteenth century.

It gleamed pearly white in the moonlight flanked by the darkness of the shrubs and trees.

Then as they waited, and the Marquis knew that Sir Algernon was anticipating the next surprise, there came the faint, sweet sound of violins from the direction of the Temple.

At first indistinct in the distance, they could now see more clearly coming towards them a number of musicians, playing as they moved a music which seemed compelling and to have a strange, stimulating note which made the pulses begin to beat quicker.

There were not only violins, which Saviya had told the Marquis they called 'bas' alja—the king of instruments—there were also the notes of the violas, the cymbals and the sitar.

They drew nearer until they were just on the edge of the lawn, and then they divided so that as a background there was the white perfection of the Greek Temple.

The music intensified, and suddenly a dancer appeared. She seemed to emerge through the music and be a part of it.

The Marquis had expected Saviya to be a remarkable dancer, but it was difficult to put into words the sheer beauty of her movements.

She was dressed in Gypsy clothes, not those she habitually wore, but those which he knew instinctively belonged to the theatre—white, embroidered with vivid colours, the sleeves of her muslin blouse puffed out almost like wings from her shoulders.

Her skirt flew out from her tiny waist and the Marquis knew it was not one skirt but seven which frothed, rustled and shimmered with every movement she made.

There were jewels around her neck which glittered in the moonlight, and on her head there was a wreath of flowers with trailing ribbons of every hue flying out behind her.

It seemed almost impossible that her feet touched the ground as she flew like a butterfly over the green grass.

Then from behind the musicians there came men and women carrying torches, which lit the garden with a strange, pagan light.

Now the music changed. It was no longer soft and entrancing but wild yet sweet; violent and yet tender; and while Saviya accelerated the speed of her movements, the Gypsies with the torches began to sing.

There was a bewildering beauty in the melody of their voices and a charm in their words, even though those listening could not understand them.

Sometimes the tone was delicate and liquid like the sound of silver bells, at other times it was a wild, invigorating and exciting tone which seemed to draw the heart of those who listened from their bodies and make them one with the music itself.

Quicker and quicker the sound rose; quicker and quicker Saviya danced. She leapt until she almost seemed to hang motionless in the air and she twirled until she no longer seemed human.

Yet everything she did had such an unbelievable

grace, so much beauty, so much haunting loveliness, that she became the embodiment of a dream.

Quicker and quicker, louder and louder the music, the dancing, until it aroused an elation that was a part not only of the body but of the very soul.

Then when it seemed that no human being could hold such intensity any longer, slowly the violence of the music was replaced by a soft rippling melody as of a quiet sea after a storm.

First the flaming torches moved away towards the Temple, then the musicians, and finally Saviya herself, dancing like a bewitching will-o'-the-wisp only half-seen in the shadow of the retreating singers—until as the music faded into the distance she stood for a moment silhouetted against the pillars of the Temple, her slight figure hardly human in its grace.

As the last lingering note of the violins died away, she too disappeared.

For a moment there was complete and absolute silence. Then Sir Algernon jumped to his feet slapping and cheering.

"Bravo! Unbelievable! Exquisite! Tremendous!" he exclaimed.

Almost as if he moved in a dream the Marquis, too, rose to applaud, but he felt somehow as if his voice was constricted in his throat.

It had been, although he hardly dared admit it to himself, an emotional experience which he had never encountered before.

Because it was difficult to find words to express what they had all felt, they moved back into the Salon almost as if the silent beauty of the night was too poignant for the commonplaces of conversation.

A little later Saviya came in.

She was still wearing the beautiful embroidered Russian dress in which she had danced and, as she entered the Salon, the Marquis crossed the room towards her and taking her hand lifted it to his lips.

"I expected you to be good," he said quietly, "but

83

I have no words to tell you how superlative you were in every way."

She smiled at him without replying and accepted the congratulations of Sir Algernon and Charles Collington.

"You realise now," the latter said to Sir Algernon, "that you owe us a thousand guineas."

"It is a price I will pay willingly just to see this lovely lady dance," Sir Algernon said. "May I know her real name?"

"It is Saviya," the Marquis answered, "and she is, as you have guessed, a Gypsy. But her mother is a Russian and a dancer."

"Tonight you recaptured for me my lost youth!" Sir Algernon said.

He smiled and added to the Marquis:

"Now you understand why, when I was talking to you before dinner, I sounded perhaps exaggeratedly enthusiastic, but even so I was under-estimating, as you must admit, the brilliance not only of the Russian singers but their dancers."

Then he asked with a note of curiosity in his voice:

"You must explain to me, Ruckley, where you found this fascinating creature. How does it happen that she is here in England?"

"An introduction was thrust upon me," the Marquis smiled.

He explained how he had run Saviya down with his Phaeton.

"If it had not happened," he finished, "I should have had no idea that the Gypsies were encamped on my land. It was not until tonight that I had even seen a sign of them."

"They are a secret people," Sir Algernon said, and turning to Saviya he asked, "are you all right after your accident? You might easily have broken your leg, and that would have been a tragedy beyond words."

"I was fortunate it was no worse," Saviya answered. "All that is left now is a small scar on my forehead and the few marks on my arm."

"It still looks rather bruised," Charles Collington said, looking down at her arm as he came and stood beside her.

She laughed.

"That is the wrong arm."

"But you do have a bruise there," he persisted.

"No," she replied. "That is a birth-mark, and it is a sign much respected by my tribe."

"Why?" Charles Collington enquired.

"Because," she replied, "it is the head of a hawk. A hawk has very sharp eyes, and this indicates that I am in fact a 'Seer.'"

"Yes, you are right," Charles Collington said, "the mark does look like a hawk's head—can you see it does, Ruckley?"

It was a birth-mark about the size of a florin and Sir Algernon looked at it. But the Marquis went to fetch Saviya a glass of wine from the side-table.

"You must be both tired and thirsty after that incredible performance," he said as he handed it to her.

"I seldom feel tired when I am dancing," she answered. "What was much more frightening was playing the part of a Lady of Quality."

"Which you did as to the manor born," Charles Collington said. "Do you not agree, Gibbon?"

"Of course I agree! It was faultless," Sir Algernon answered. "I am only so disappointed that I shall not be able to give you dinner in London next week."

"I must say, Gibbon, you are taking the loss of a thousand guineas like a sportsman," Charles Collington said irrepressibly. "I almost feel embarrassed at winning the money."

They all laughed at this. Then the Marquis raising his glass said:

"I want to drink to Saviya. There is no-one who has surprised us more with her amazing talents, or who could have been more modest about them. She told me she was a dancer, but not for one moment did I expect a performance such as the one we have just witnessed."

"What I cannot understand," Sir Algernon said, "is why you are here; why you do not stay in St. Petersburg where your talents would be appreciated?"

"My father, like all Gypsies, has a wanderlust," Saviya answered. "After a little while—however comfortable we may be, however happy—he wants to move on. We wandered all over Russia from the North to the very South, then he had a yearning to see England again."

"He has been here before?" the Marquis asked.

"Yes, but many years ago," Saviya replied, "before I was born, or when I was only a baby. I do not remember it."

They talked for some time and then Saviya said:

"I think I must go. My father will wonder what has happened to me, since the rest of the tribe will have long returned to the camp."

As she spoke the door opened and a footman came into the Salon. He carried something in his hand and went up to stand at the side of the Marquis waiting for him to finish speaking.

"What is it?" the Marquis asked.

"This has just been left at the front door, M'Lord. A man gave it to me saying I was to present it to Your Lordship in your bed-room, but seeing that you had not retired, I thought I should bring it here."

"A man?" the Marquis questioned.

"I think he must have been a Gypsy, M'Lord. He said, 'Tell His Lordship this is a gift from the Gypsies.'"

The Marquis glanced at Saviya.

"It sounds as if your father is being unexpectedly generous."

The footman put the parcel into his hands and Saviya saw it was a round wicker basket, not very large, the lid fastened down at each side with a small wooden peg slipped into a cane loop.

"Do you know anything about this?" the Marquis enquired.

She shook her head.

"I cannot imagine what it is. I do not think it can be from my father. It is not the sort of thing he would do without telling me."

"A gift from the Gypsies . . ." the Marquis repeated. "Well, I shall expect something unusual, Saviya."

He pulled out the two small wooden pegs as he spoke.

Then, just as he was about to raise the lid, Saviya suddenly seized it from his hands, and with a swiftness that took him by surprise, ran down the room, put the basket on the floor and pushed it away from her.

It slid across the polished parquet floor, where there were no rugs, to come to rest almost in front of the door.

"Whatever are you doing?" the Marquis asked in astonishment.

As he spoke, the lid of the basket slipped to one side, and through the aperture came first a long, forked tongue, then the head and finally the body of a snake!

It moved so quickly there was hardly time for anyone to ejaculate before on reaching the floor it raised itself and its hood expanded to reveal that it was a cobra.

"Good God!"

The Marquis could hardly say the words, while Charles Collington exclaimed:

"A pistol! Where do you keep a pistol, Fabius?"

The cobra darted its head first right and then left. It was hissing, its long tongue licking in and out of its mouth, obviously angry and annoyed at being moved about.

Charles Collington started to walk cautiously along the side of the room in an attempt to reach the door behind the snake. With a little gesture of her hand, Saviya stopped him.

"Keep still!" she said in a very low voice. "Do not move or speak."

There was an authority in her tone that was unmistakable, and while the Marquis would have expostulated, he bit back the words even as he started to say them.

Moving a little nearer to the hissing, angry reptile, Saviya started to make a strange sound.

It was not exactly singing, it was like the notes of the reed-pipe used by the snake-charmers in India. Yet it came from between her lips and was at first so faint that the three men listening could hardly hear it.

But the cobra heard and now its tongue no longer flicked out, and it turned its head curiously, first this way, then that, regarding Saviya with its yellow eyes.

He was still poised for the attack, his head with its inflated hood high in the air.

Slowly, making that strange music which seemed to consist of just three notes repeated over and over again, Saviya drew a little nearer.

Firstly, she sank down on her knees just a short distance from the cobra, her eyes on his, her body very still.

There was complete silence in the room except for her voice, and the three men watching hardly seemed to breathe. They stood as if turned to stone.

Then slowly, almost imperceptibly, in time to the notes, Saviya began to move her shoulders a little to the left and then to the right, swaying rhythmically, her eyes all the time on the cobra.

Now he too began to move, swaying as she did, turning his yellowish head with the black and white spectacle-shaped markings on its wide hood to the right, to the left, to the right, to the left.

Still she intensified her tune and her movements until, its hood subsiding, the cobra sank little by little, lower and lower until finally his head was flat on the ground and he appeared to make an obeisance to her.

Then her tune altered and, almost as if she gave a note of command, the sound was abrupt yet still melodious.

Unbelievably, as it seemed to the men watching, the cobra obeyed, and turning he slithered slowly, moving in a very different manner to the quickness with which he had left the basket, back into it.

He slipped over the edge of the basket and, as they watched, his long dark body slithered after his head until finally the tip of his tail disappeared.

Still singing, Saviya very gently moved forward. She pressed the lid back into place and slipped the wooden pegs into the cane loops, which held it firm.

As soon as the basket was secure she ceased her song, and it seemed for a moment as if she would collapse.

The Marquis was at her side and put his arms around her to lift her to her feet.

"Are you all right?" he asked.

"I . . . I am . . . all right."

But he saw that her face was very pale and was afraid that she might faint.

He helped her across the room to settle her down into a chair.

"Do not talk!" he commanded and poured her out a drink.

She took two or three sips, then gave him back the glass.

"I do not need it," she said.

"How could you charm that snake?" Sir Algernon enquired. "I have heard of it being done, but would never have believed it was possible for anyone without an enormous amount of training, and certainly not for a woman!"

"I have seen it done many times," Saviya replied. "But it is the first time I have actually tried it myself."

"Then it was even more miraculous," the Marquis said. "We can only thank you very gratefully, Saviya. I do not need to tell you that you saved my life!"

Saviya gave a deep sigh.

"I suddenly realised that the basket was not of the type used by Gypsies, but by the Circus people. For a moment I could not think where I had seen one before, then I remembered the snake-charmers that we have encountered on our travels."

She paused for a moment before looking up at the Marquis and said:

"Their snakes usually have the bags of venom in their fangs removed, but this was a young cobra and had not been treated. If he had bitten you, it would have been fatal. The venom acts quickly on the nervous system."

"But who can want to murder you, Ruckley?" Sir Algernon enquired.

"The answer to that is quite easy—" Charles Collington began, only to be silenced as the Marquis interposed:

"There is no point in discussing it, Charles. Again we have no proof."

"What is going on? You must tell me about it," Sir Algernon asked curiously.

"I think it is time that Saviya went to bed," the Marquis suggested.

"Yes, I must go," she agreed obediently.

She curtsied to Sir Algernon and to Charles Collington. The Marquis walked with her across the Hall and out through the main door.

She turned to say good-night but he shook his head.

"I will come with you to the wood," he said. "I do not like to think of your going alone."

"I will be quite safe," she replied. "It is you I worry about. Who is the man who wishes to kill you? If you do not tell me I shall lie awake all night trying to see his name as I have seen his face."

"You told me when we were in the Picture Gallery that his name began with the same letter as mine," the Marquis replied. "You were right, Saviya, he is my cousin, Jethro Ruck. If I am dead he will inherit the title and the Estate."

"This is not the first time he has tried?" Saviya enquired, as they walked across the Court-Yard side by side.

"He attempted to destroy me in London, by dislodging a piece of masonry from the top of my house in Berkeley Square," the Marquis answered. "It missed me by a hair's breadth, and tonight if I had, as he thought, retired to bed I would have opened the basket when I was alone."

Saviya shivered.

"He is dangerous! Very dangerous!" she said. "I beg you to be careful."

The Marquis smiled.

"You sound very like Charles. You tell me to be careful, but I should require to be as clairvoyant as you are to anticipate the strange and unusual ways in which Jethro is attempting to exterminate me."

The Marquis was silent for a moment and then he said:

"It was clever of him to pretend it was a present from the Gypsies. He must have learnt about you when he was making enquiries in the village, and he knew, I dare say, without being told that if I did in fact receive a present from you I would open it personally."

"I will never send you anything that you do not anticipate," Saviya promised.

"I doubt if Jethro will repeat the same trick twice. What shall I do with the snake—kill it?"

"No!" Saviya said. "I think it is wrong to take life unless it is absolutely necessary. But the Kalderash celebrate the Feast of the Serpent on March fifteenth. On that day, if anyone kills a snake, he will be fortunate throughout the year."

She paused before she continued:

"I have heard there is a Circus at St. Albans. That was where your cousin must have obtained the snake. Send them back the cobra with your compliments. I think they will understand and not make the mistake another time of selling their stock to an outsider."

"I will do that," the Marquis said. "At the same time I think it is being very magnanimous. If I had any sense I would send it back to Jethro himself."

He gave a short laugh.

"The trouble is, if it killed him, I should have a lot of explaining to do, and there is no proof that it was his idea in the first place."

"You must be on your guard."

"I have a feeling I shall be safe as long as you are here with me," the Marquis answered.

By this time they had reached the edge of the wood and Saviya stopped.

"There is no reason for you to come any further."

"There is every reason I should protect you," the Marquis replied, "but if you would rather go alone, I will respect your wishes."

"Thank you!" she said softly.

"I have so much to thank you for. First for the moments of unbelievable beauty you showed me to-night—and secondly for saving my life!"

He put out his right hand as he spoke and she laid her left hand in it.

Their palms touched. Then a sudden streak of ecstasy, a thrill such as he had never known in his whole life, swept through the Marquis and he knew as he looked down into Saviya's eyes that she felt the same.

For a moment neither of them could move, and yet it was almost as if they lay close against each other and were one.

"Saviya! You know what I feel about you?" the Marquis said hoarsely.

She did not answer and he saw her eyes were searching his.

"I want you!" he said. "I want you more than I have ever wanted anything in my life. Come with me, Saviya! I will give you everything you can ever desire and we will be very happy together."

She did not answer until at last she said in a low voice he could hardly hear:

"Are you asking me to be your *Piramni?*"

The Marquis had no need of a translation of her meaning.

"Must we have words for something that is so wonderful, so beautiful?" he asked. "We were made for each other, Saviya. I have known these past few days that you were aware of me. I could feel it whenever we were near each other. I could see it in your eyes."

She turned her head a little away from him and he said:

"It is too late, my darling, to pretend. I think you love me a little, and I can make you love me with all the wild wonder that lies within your exquisite body, and your entrancing brain. Come to me, Saviya! We shall find a happiness which is granted to few people."

She raised her head.

"I . . . cannot! You know I . . . cannot!"

"Why?"

"Because it would be . . . wrong."

"Who is to decide that?" the Marquis asked roughly. "You may have tribal laws, Saviya, but they are not the laws either of this country or of the Church. Forget them! Remember only that you are a woman and I am a man. We belong to each other!"

His fingers tightened as he went on:

"I will look after you and you shall never want for the whole of your life. That I swear! But do not let us throw away this wonderful, this perfect happiness which we feel when we are together."

She did not reply, yet he knew without being told she was not convinced.

"Look at me, Saviya!"

She hesitated and then as if she must obey him she threw back her head. Her worried eyes were very large in her small face.

"You love me!" the Marquis said. "I know you love me and you thrill me in a way I have never known in my whole life before! My body aches for you! I desire you, Saviya, but there is so much more to it than that. I want to be with you; to know you are there; to

93

listen to your voice. I want to watch the movement of
your lips; to see that strange, lovely, melting expression in your eyes which tells me that you love me."

Saviya drew in her breath. Her lips were parted a
little, her eyes were pools of mystery and the Marquis knew she was trembling.

"God, I want you!"

It seemed with the words as if something broke
within him. He swept her into his arms. He held her
crushingly against him.

His lips were on hers and then as her head fell
back against his shoulder, his kiss was not only demanding and possessive, but gentle, as he realised how
soft, small and yielding she was.

It was a moment of magic such as he had never
imagined. It seemed as if the whole world stood still
and they were alone in an eternity where there was
nothing but themselves.

"I love you!" He remembered even as he spoke, that
he had never in his life said that to a woman.

"Me hamava Tut!" she whispered.

He knew that she was saying the same words as he
had said to her, but in Romany.

"I love you!—I love you!"

Now he kissed her eyes; her cheeks; the little pulse
throbbing frantically in her throat; and then again her
lips.

"Come back with me now!" he begged. "Why should
we wait? I want you with me! I cannot wait until
tomorrow to see you again!"

Very slowly she drew herself away from him.

Her face in the moonlight was radiant. Then he saw
her expression change.

"No!" she said. "No! No! It is . . . wrong not only
for me but for . . . you. I love you too much to . . .
hurt you!"

"Why should it hurt me?" the Marquis asked roughly.

She stood looking at him and he felt once again in

that strange way he had felt once before that she was not looking at him, but through and beyond him.

"It is you who . . . matters," she said softly.

Then before he could stop her, before he could take her again into his arms, she had moved away from him amongst the tree trunks and vanished!

"Saviya!" he called desperately. "Saviya!"

But there was no answer from the darkness. He was alone.

Chapter Five

The Marquis walked slowly back to the house, and after a short conversation with Sir Algernon and Charles Collington he retired to bed.

He gave orders to Bush before he did so that, as Saviya had suggested, the snake should be sent over to the St. Albans Circus the following morning in charge of a groom.

When Hobley left him he sat for some time in an arm-chair before getting into bed, and found himself recapturing the incredible magic of the evening.

He had known as he watched Saviya dance that his whole being responded, and she made him feel as no woman had ever done before.

Then when he touched her and was aware of a new rapture and ecstasy within himself, he knew he was in love.

There had been many women in his life whom he had found amusing, entertaining and at times irresistible, but never had they fulfilled his first expectation. Always he had found, however enticing they might be, they could not give him what he really wanted from a woman.

This was something he could not express even to himself. He just knew there was some hidden part of his being that remained untouched by even the most alluring and attractive woman, so that in some inexplicable manner she failed him.

He had laughed at love, mocked it and declared it

was the infatuation of fools, but there was nevertheless an idealism that told him that true love was possible, even if he had not met it.

He understood now why Eurydice had been prepared to give up everything that was familiar and
cross the world to a strange land with a man of whom
she knew little, but whom she loved.

She had warned him that one day he would feel
the same, but even as he thought of her words, he
knew it was impossible for him to offer Saviya marriage.

It was what he should do. Even while to her he
was a "Gorgio," she would wish him to want her to be
his wife. Yet how could he make her the Marchioness
of Ruckley?

He told himself that, where only he was concerned,
he could not think of anyone more suitable and indeed more perfect to be his wife and the Chatelaine
of his house.

But he would have been a fool if he had not realised the difficulties, and indeed the unhappiness such
a position would entail for Saviya herself.

However lovely she was, however competent, however charming, she would have to endure the sneers,
the innuendos and the insults that she would receive
not only from his friends but, in a way far more important, from those he employed and who were part
of his background.

Saviya might have charmed the servants when she
stayed in the House, but would they accept her as
their Mistress?

And even if the servants could be captivated, what
about the keepers, the other employees on the Estate,
the people in the village, the farmers, the tenants and
everyone who lived in the immediate neighbourhood
of Ruckley, who had looked up to the family and respected them for generations.

Hatred and fear of the Gypsies lay deep in the
roots of almost all Englishmen, but why it should be so
the Marquis could not understand.

Ever since the Gypsies had first come to the country in 1512, there had been people who not only disliked them but who attempted to persecute them.

In the book by John Howland which The Reverend had found in the Library, the Marquis had read that even in the reign of Henry VIII a number of outlandish people calling themselves Egyptians had been reshipped to France at public expense.

In the "31st yeare of the Raigne of our Souraigne Lady, the Queen's Majestie, Acts were passed for the punishinge and suppressinge of Roags and Vacabonds," mentioning particular parts of the country where the Gypsies congregated.

Under Scottish laws in 1609, "Sorners, common thieves, commonly called Egyptians were directed to pass forth of the Kingdom under pain of death as common, notorious and condemned thieves."

Things had altered very little, the Marquis thought, and despite a number of romantic writers who had glamourised the Gypsies, the country people still believed they could curse their crops or their animals, cast the "Evil Eye," and that Gypsies were, in the main, evil folk.

According to Howland there were some thirty-six thousand Gypsies in Great Britain and yet nothing was done for them.

No attempt was made to educate their children, Clergymen avoided the camps, and they received severe sentences whenever they were brought in front of the Magistrates.

And yet, the Marquis thought, there were Gypsies like Saviya, who was more intelligent than any woman he had ever met and certainly more cultured than the majority of his friends.

It was true she was half-Russian and, according to Sir Algernon, the Russians were different from those in the rest of Europe. But socially she would always be tainted by her Gypsy blood.

He wondered if any marriage could survive when a man must be continually on the defensive to protect

99

his wife, not against violence, but slanderous tongues and evil minds.

No. Marriage was impossible! It therefore remained, the Marquis thought, to persuade Saviya to live with him as his mistress.

He had not missed the contempt in her voice when she had said the word *"Piramni,"* and he had known that to her it suggested much worse sin than it would have to an Englishwoman.

The strict morality of the Gypsies was part of their faith, an intrinsic part of their way of life, and he knew that only a great love utterly beyond self would make Saviya accept a position that offended every instinct in her body.

But what else could he do? He asked himself the question and then, because there was no answer, he at last went to bed.

He found it impossible to sleep, and rose very early.

He had a feeling it was urgent for him to see Saviya as soon as possible. There had been something unsatisfactory and indecisive in the manner in which she had left him last night, after that moment of indescribable wonder when he had held her in his arms and kissed her.

He knew irrefutably it was the first kiss she had ever received.

He was aware as he felt her quivering against him that he had aroused in her a rapture to equal his own and that already, without physical possession, they were one in body, mind and soul.

'I love her!' the Marquis told himself, and he knew it was an expression of the deepest feelings of which he was capable.

He felt sure she would come to the House at her usual time, which was about eleven o'clock.

Invariably when he returned from dealing with Eurydice's Estate, he would find her in the Library with The Reverend.

She would be discussing subjects so erudite he thought them beyond the intelligence of a woman, and looking so entrancingly beautiful that it was hard to believe she could be as clever as The Reverend proclaimed her to be.

Today the Marquis thought he could not bear to miss a moment of the time they might be together. So this morning Saviya would not be waiting for him, but he for Saviya.

As Hobley assisted him into his riding-clothes, he remembered that he had not given Saviya back the coins that she had borrowed from her father for them to deceive Sir Algernon.

He must remember, he thought, to return them as they were in fact extremely valuable.

How strange it must be, he thought to himself, to know that one must wander the world encountering terrible discomforts from the climate, the hostility of the different races and enduring all sorts of privations, when in fact one could well afford to settle down in comparative comfort.

Then with a smile he felt it undoubtedly had its compensations for a man. To battle against tremendous odds was a challenge. It must also be a very successful way of avoiding boredom and social ennui, when the horizon was limitless.

"Do you know what time Sir Algernon and Captain Collington plan to leave for London, Hobley?" he asked his Valet.

"Sir Algernon ordered his carriage for eleven o'clock, M'Lord."

"I will be back long before that," the Marquis said. "There are certain people I have to see on Lady Walden's Estate. But will you assure Sir Algernon and Captain Collington I shall not be long delayed and hope to be with them some time before their departure?"

"I'll give them your message, M'Lord."

"I have discovered a quick way to the new land, Hobley," the Marquis said with satisfaction, as the Valet helped him into his riding-coat.

"Indeed, M'Lord?"

"I have been using it now for the past week. I have timed myself and it takes me not quite twenty minutes."

"Riding the finest horse-flesh, M'Lord," Hobley said with a smile.

"I admit a fine mount is essential," the Marquis replied.

"I think I know the way you mean, M'Lord," Hobley said. "It is through the Ride at the north end of Battle Wood."

"That is right," the Marquis replied. "It takes me directly onto the parkland sloping down to Lady Walden's house."

The Marquis took a quick glance at himself in the mirror and went from the room.

Hobley watched him appreciatively as he walked down the passage.

There was no-one, he thought, who could look smarter than his master in a grey whipcord riding-coat, which had been cut by a master-hand, over a yellow waistcoat above the spotless white of his riding-breeches.

The shine on the Marquis's riding-boots was Hobley's special pride.

He had refused innumerable bribes to tell the secret of their brilliance to the London Dandies who tried to imitate the Marquis's elegance, and who invariably failed in their aspirations.

Outside the front door two grooms were holding with some difficulty a stallion the Marquis had acquired only a month ago from Tattersall's salesrooms.

It was a fiery young horse with a touch of Arab in its pedigree, and as the Marquis swung himself into the saddle he thought with pleasure that his ride was not going to be an easy one. He would have to assert his mastery over an animal that was not yet broken to his touch.

The stallion bucked several times to show its independence, and was checked from starting off at too swift a pace.

Finally he contented himself with shying at several imaginary objects before the Marquis allowed him to trot over the Park towards the woods.

As he went the Marquis thought of how last night he had walked in the moonlight with Saviya.

It was impossible to keep her from his thoughts. Just to think of her eyes raised to his, of her softness as she had surrendered herself into his arms, made his breath come quicker.

Also he felt once again that strange constriction within his heart that he had never known before.

"God, she is beautiful!" he told himself.

It was not only her beauty which held him. There was some indefinable link between them, some union that had made them part of each other from the first moment they had met.

"I want her!" the Marquis said beneath his breath. "Dear God, how I want her!"

The stallion distracted his attention from Saviya by shying at one of the speckled deer which, startled at their approach, ran from beneath a tree.

Already they had reached the woods which on the north side of the house constituted a background, and a wind-break had been planned for the great red-brick mansion when it was first erected.

There was, as the Marquis had told Hobley, a Ride through the wood which had been cut originally by the tree-fellers so that they would use it for conveying the chopped wood to the House in their carts.

Now it was a straight lane through the trees, and the Marquis set his horse to a gallop putting up his hand as he did so to settle his hat more firmly upon his head.

The great trees, many of them centuries old, rose high on either side. As it was so early in the morning, the sun was not yet strong enough to percolate through the branches and dry up the dew, which lay like small diamonds on the grass.

There was a scent of pine and of birchwood, and

103

among the trees there was an occasional glimpse of the vivid blue of bluebells.

Then as the stallion increased his pace the Marquis, enjoying a sense of satisfaction and well-being, quite suddenly and unexpectedly, even as he reached it, saw something rising from the ground with a quick movement.

It was a rope! Knee-high it was taut in front of his horse.

There was not even time for the Marquis to tighten the reins before he felt his mount gallop straight into it, heard himself shout, and knew, even as he fell, there was nothing he could do.

He was conscious of the violent impact as his head hit the ground, then he thought he heard the bone snap as his collar-bone broke . . .

Someone was speaking very softly and there was a touch on his forehead that was soothing and somehow hypnotic.

"Go to sleep!" the soft voice said. "You are dreaming. Go to sleep!"

The cool fingers were comforting, and yet vaguely the Marquis remembered that someone had been crying out . . . There had been darkness and pain . . .

But he could not ignore the compelling movement on his forehead, and he fell asleep.

Slowly he came back to consciousness . . .

He thought for a moment he was with his mother. He was in someone's arms and his head was against the softness of a woman's breast. Then he was aware of a fragrance.

He was very comfortable. He felt secure and there was a strange happiness in knowing he was loved.

Again he thought of his mother, but the fragrance haunted him.

He remembered now he had smelt it first in the hair of a Gypsy he had carried in his arms after he had run her down with his Phaeton.

He felt very weak. It was too much trouble to open his eyes. Then he felt whoever held him move, and he wanted to cry out because his cheek no longer rested against the softness of a breast.

Instead his head was on a pillow, and he felt as if he had been deprived of something very precious.

"How is he, Miss?"

The Marquis thought he would have known Hobley's voice anywhere, even though he spoke in a whisper.

"He was not so restless in the night, but he has not yet regained consciousness."

It was Saviya who spoke. Who else could speak in that soft, melodious tone with just the trace of a foreign accent?

With an effort, feeling as if his eyelids were weighted down with lead, the Marquis opened his eyes.

She must have been looking at him, for with a little cry Saviya knelt beside him. He felt her hand against his cheek.

"You are awake!"

The Marquis looked at her. Her face was very near to his, and he could see the worry and at the same time a glint of excitement in her eyes.

"What—happened?" he asked.

Even as he spoke he remembered the rope across the ride. He had fallen!

"I do not think you ought to talk."

"I want to—know what—happened," the Marquis repeated and now his voice was stronger.

As he spoke, he realised that he was lying on a bed that was almost on the floor and that he was enclosed by curved walls so that he thought for a moment he was in a cave.

It was so small there was hardly room for himself, for Saviya kneeling beside him, and for Hobley with his head bent just inside what appeared to be an open door.

"Where am—I?" the Marquis asked.

"You're all right, M'Lord, and that's thanks to Miss Saviya," Hobley replied. "It's worried we've been about you and that's the truth."

With an effort the Marquis turned his head a little, realised that his shoulder was bandaged. He remembered breaking his collar-bone.

"I fell, but it was not my horse's fault. Is he all right?"

"He went home," Saviya said. "There was a rope stretched between two trees. The men raised it just as you reached them."

"What men?" the Marquis asked, and knew even as he spoke it was an unnecessary question.

"Mr. Jethro's men, M'Lord," Hobley said bitterly, "and 'twas them that swore false witness in front of the Magistrates against Miss Saviya."

The Marquis suddenly felt more awake. He tried to raise himself a little and then was conscious of a sharp pain in his back.

"Do not move," Saviya said quickly, "they stabbed you!"

"They'd have killed you, M'Lord, if Miss Saviya hadn't come along when she did," Hobley said.

"I have to know what happened," the Marquis said, with some of his old authority back in his voice. "Start at the beginning."

Saviya looked at Hobley as if for guidance.

"It'll worry His Lordship," he said to her, "if we don't tell him."

"It will indeed," the Marquis affirmed. "All I can remember is feeling myself fall, and knowing it was a rope against my horse's knees that had been the cause."

"'Tis an old trick, M'Lord, but a clever one," Hobley said. "They must've known Your Lordship went that way every morning and were lying in wait for you."

"I had a feeling that something was wrong," Saviya said. "We were packing up ready to move on . . ."

"You were leaving?" the Marquis interrupted.

106

He looked at her and her eyes fell before his.

"I had to . . . go," she murmured, and he thought the colour rose in her cheeks.

"But you stayed!"

"I felt that you were in danger, and then to make sure it was just my imagination, I told one of the Gypsies to bring me a horse and to come with me on another."

She gave a little sigh.

"I thought as it was so early that you would not yet have left the House, and I intended merely to watch you cross the Park, pass into the Ride and out the other side."

"You have watched me before!" the Marquis said with a sudden perception.

Again the colour seemed to tinge her cheeks.

"Almost . . . every morning," she answered.

"It was fortunate, M'Lord," Hobley interposed, "that Miss Saviya saw you just as you disappeared into the Ride. If she hadn't done so, you wouldn't be lying here at this moment!"

"What happened?" the Marquis asked.

As he spoke, he covered Saviya's hand with his own and felt her fingers tremble beneath his.

"As I reached the Ride," Saviya said, "I actually saw your horse tripped and you shoot over its head. Then when you were on the ground, two men emerged from behind the trees. One of them held a long knife like a dagger in his hand. Before I could move nearer or shout, he drove it into your back."

The Marquis understood then the reason for the pain he had felt a few moments before when he had tried to raise himself.

"The man drew out the knife and would have stabbed you again," Saviya said, "if I had not urged my horse forward, shouting at the top of my voice. And the Gypsy boy with me did the same. The noise we made frightened the two men and they ran away into the woods."

She drew in her breath before she said:

"When I reached you I thought at first you were dead!"

"It's lucky you aren't, M'Lord," Hobley said. "An inch or two lower and there's no doubt those murdering devils would have achieved their object."

"What did you do?" the Marquis asked, holding Saviya's hand a little more tightly.

"Yerko—the Gypsy who came with me—and I carried your body away into the trees in case the men should return to try to finish murdering you."

She smiled.

"You are very heavy, My Lord."

"How did you manage it?" he asked.

"Yerko is strong and I wanted to save you," she said simply.

"When a Gypsy came to the House to tell me I was urgently needed by Miss Saviya in the wood, I'd a suspicion that something like this had happened," Hobley said. "I was sure, M'Lord, that Mr. Jethro was up to something when he was seen at The Green Man."

"Is there any proof that it was Mr. Jethro who tried to kill me?" the Marquis asked.

Saviya looked at Hobley and neither of them spoke. The Marquis knew they were wondering whether they should tell him the truth.

"Dammit all!" he said, "I am not a child. Tell me what has happened."

Saviya put her hand on his forehead.

"You have been running a very high fever for a long time," she said, "and we do not wish to agitate you."

"It will agitate me a great deal if I think you are keeping something from me," the Marquis said.

"Very well, M'Lord, you'd best know the worst," Hobley said. "There is a warrant out for Miss Saviya's arrest for having killed you. The knife that them murderers used on you is in the hands of the Magistrate, and Mr. Jethro has moved into the House!"

"God dammit!" the Marquis ejaculated.

He attempted to move again but there was a sharp pain in his back which brought beads of sweat onto his forehead.

"This is too much for you," Saviya said. "You should have waited. There is no hurry for you to learn these unpleasant things."

"No hurry?" the Marquis enquired. "How long have I been here?"

"For over a week," Saviya answered.

"For over a week?" the Marquis could hardly repeat the words.

"Time enough, M'Lord, for Mr. Jethro to assert that you've been murdered by Miss Saviya, that the Gypsies have buried your body, and that he's entitled to assume both the title and the ownership of the Estates!"

The Marquis lay for a moment in silence trying to digest the enormity of what Hobley had told him.

Then he asked:

"Why has no-one searched for me?"

"Because if you had been taken back to the House in the state you were in," Saviya said, "I am certain that your cousin would have found some way of disposing of you when you were too weak to resist him."

"Besides," Hobley said, "with a warrant out for her arrest, if Miss Saviya is seen she will be taken to prison."

"Where am I hidden?" the Marquis asked.

"In my caravan in the very depths of the forest," Saviya answered. "If it seems dark, it is because the Gypsies have draped it with shrubs and ivy so that it is almost impossible for anyone to see it, even if they are just outside."

"That's true enough, M'Lord," Hobley agreed. "When I come here I often wonder whether Miss Saviya has whisked Your Lordship away in the night, even when the caravan is almost right in front of my face."

"And your people, they are all right?" the Marquis asked.

"They have moved so that it is more difficult to find them," Saviya replied. "But, as you can imagine, your cousin is not making too close a search for you . . . or for me. The last thing he wants is for anyone to contend that his bribed confederates are not telling the truth."

"I will not have him taking my place!" the Marquis said in what he meant to be an angry and determined tone.

But even to himself his voice sounded very weak and before he could say any more he fell asleep . . .

It was two days later before the Marquis could grasp all the details of the drama that Jethro had planned so cleverly, or appreciate that had Saviya not been watching him ride through the wood, he would in fact have been found dead in the Ride with a Gypsy's knife between his shoulder-blades.

"The knife even had Gypsy characters on it," Saviya said, "and I think that either it must have come from the Circus folk from whom your cousin obtained the cobra, or he bought it in a Curiosity Shop in London."

"But is it a Gypsy knife?"

"A description of it was in the newspapers," Saviya said, "and my father thinks it is a Spanish dagger such as the Gitanos carry and use in their quarrels."

"Good circumstantial evidence," the Marquis remarked.

It was Hobley who told him how arrogant and autocratic his cousin was being at Ruckley House.

"Sir Algernon went back to London, M'Lord, after Mr. Jethro had arrived, saying he'd heard a strange story in the village that two men had seen you brought down by an ambush and then being stabbed by a Gypsy woman."

Hobley's voice was contemptuous as he continued: "They had the rope as evidence, and said they

110

were walking through the Ride as they were looking for work at one of the adjacent farms. They had their story very pat, 'twas difficult to fault them."

"Jethro would have seen to that!" the Marquis murmured.

"Mr. Jethro's clever, M'Lord. Make no mistake about that!"

"I am not!" the Marquis answered. "Go on, Hobley."

"Mr. Jethro was obviously so pleased to relate such a gruesome tale that Sir Algernon, while expressing his deep concern that Your Lordship had disappeared, said he thought the whole thing a bundle of lies and, from what he'd seen of Miss Saviya, she'd murder nobody, least of all you."

"Yet he did not wish to be involved," the Marquis said with a smile.

"That was obvious, M'Lord. But Captain Collington argued fiercely with Mr. Jethro."

"I can imagine him doing that!" the Marquis remarked.

"He stayed one more night, saying he was going to search for you. In fact he came looking in the woods, and then Mr. Jethro ordered him out of the House."

"He actually did that?" the Marquis ejaculated.

"Yes, M'Lord. He said as the new Marquis of Ruckley he wasn't standing for the Captain's impudence, and he certainly didn't intend to offer him any further hospitality!"

The Marquis would have expressed himself forcefully but Saviya interposed:

"You promised you would not get angry. It is bad for you. If you do not listen quietly, we will tell you no more."

"Are you bullying me?" the Marquis enquired.

"I am trying to look after you for your own good," she replied.

The frown on the Marquis's forehead was replaced by a smile.

"Once again I have to thank you for saving my life," he said.

"It was Miss Saviya, M'Lord," Hobley went on, "who insisted I shouldn't join you here as I wished to do, but come backwards and forwards from the House."

"I thought that when you were better Hobley would be able to keep you informed as to what was happening," Saviya explained. "But I could not have set your collar-bone as he did, and I have to admit that the healing herbs and balms he has used on your wound were more efficacious than those we Gypsies have used for centuries."

"Mine are also based on country lore and, like the Gypsies, I'm aware that Nature knows best," Hobley said.

"I am well enough now to go and confront my cousin and expose his lies," the Marquis declared.

Both Saviya and Hobley gave a cry of disapproval.

"You will not move from here until we are sure you are strong enough," Saviya said. "Remember, he will not give in easily. He will try again to kill you."

There was so much distress in her tone that the Marquis replied:

"I will be sensible. I will not attempt anything fool-hardy—that I promise!"

"You do not know how frightened we have been about you," Saviya murmured in a low voice, and the Marquis saw the sudden glisten of tears in her eyes.

"I will not do anything stupid," he promised, "but once I am strong I intend to teach my cousin a lesson he will not forget, and I have also to clear your name, Saviya."

"That is not important," she said. "The fact that I am a murderer is just what people would expect from a Gypsy."

"There's no-one in the House as would believe that of you, Miss Saviya," Hobley assured her.

She flashed him a smile.

"Thank you."

"Mr. Jethro is not making changes in the household?" the Marquis asked and his voice was sharp.

"Not yet, M'Lord," Hobley answered, "though he threatens to do so. But the Trustees have told him that they are not prepared as yet to presume Your Lordship's death. I think it is Captain Collington who has persuaded them that there may be a chance of your survival."

"Captain Collington would never believe that Miss Saviya was capable of killing me, and he knows of the other two attempts that Mr. Jethro has made on my life."

"I believe he has informed the Trustees of what happened in Berkeley Square and about the cobra, M'Lord."

As Hobley spoke, he drew his watch from his pocket.

"I'd best be getting back, M'Lord. I've to be careful in case Mr. Jethro is suspicious or gets someone to watch my movements."

"Then do not let him suspect you," the Marquis said.

"It's why I usually take a circuitous route to get here, M'Lord," Hobley replied, "but unfortunately it takes longer."

"I am sure the exercise is good for you!" the Marquis said with a smile.

"I'd be willing to climb mountains, M'Lord, to see you back on your feet again. We miss you up at the House."

"Thank you, Hobley. It will not be long now," the Marquis smiled.

Every time he came, Hobley brought with him everything which could be carried in a basket. Food, bottles of the Marquis's favourite wine, clean linen, lotions to heal the Marquis's back, and of course the toilet requisites His Lordship always used.

The Marquis's gold hair-brushes bearing his monogram under a diamond coronet looked strangely out of place in Saviya's caravan. Yet he had not imagined how comfortable such a small place could be.

Because he was so tall, his bed took up the whole

of one side of it but there were hooks, shelves and small cupboards on all the walls, and things were stored away ingeniously in a manner which never ceased to amaze him.

The walls were painted with skilful artistry and in gay colours depicting flowers, birds, and butterflies.

The work was, however, more Russian than English, and Saviya told him that the exterior of the caravan was decorated in the same manner.

There were two windows through which, unfortunately, little light could percolate, because the caravan was draped with greenery so that it would not be seen.

But sunlight came through the open door, and at night the Marquis could see shafts of silver moonlight, which somehow reminded him of Saviya's dancing, penetrating through the thick branches of the trees.

Since he had regained consciousness, Saviya did not stay with him at night but disappeared.

He imagined she went back to her family or perhaps slept in the wood, but she was not very communicative on the subject and he did not press her.

After she had given him supper and they talked for a little while, she would merely say softly:

"It is time you went to sleep."

He would kiss her hand then she would leave him alone with his thoughts. At first he was usually so tired that he fell into a deep slumber and did not awake until the following morning, when she brought him breakfast.

Hobley washed, shaved and attended to him two or three times a day. Sometimes, if Mr. Jethro was not at the house, he would remain in the vicinity without returning home, but on other occasions he would slip in for an hour in the morning, again at luncheon time, and back again in the evening.

It was for the Marquis an unusual, strange mode of existence and yet he knew he had never been happier.

He did not feel restless and was not in the least bored.

Sometimes he would lie for a long time without speaking, watching Saviya's face as she sat in the doorway of the caravan.

He thought that her beauty was like some exquisite, exotic flower that every day unfolded more of its petals to reveal a hidden loveliness which grew more and more entrancing.

The Marquis had been in the caravan for over two weeks, when one afternoon after Hobley had returned to the house he said to Saviya:

"Soon I shall be strong enough to confront Jethro, and then you will be unable to stop me."

"You are very much better," Saviya said with a smile.

"Hobley is delighted with my collar-bone, the bandages come off tomorrow and I have very little pain in my back."

"The wound is healing quickly because you were so well," Saviya murmured, "an unhealthy man would have taken much longer."

"Before I leave this idyllic existence," the Marquis said, "we have to talk about each other, Saviya."

She stiffened and the expression on her face changed.

"You have not yet told me why on the morning that you saved my life you were leaving."

She hesitated and looked away from him.

"I told you how much I wanted you," the Marquis said. "How could you leave me, Saviya, knowing it might have been impossible for me ever to find you again?"

"It would not have been right for me to stay with you," she answered.

"Right for whom?" the Marquis asked almost angrily. "I thought you understood that I cannot live without you, Saviya. I knew it then, but now there is no doubt in my mind that we are in fact a part of each

115

other. How can you deny anything that is so perfect; so utterly and completely wonderful?"

She looked away from him and he saw that she was trembling.

"Come here, Saviya!" he said, "I want you."

He thought she would refuse him but, almost like a child who obeys the voice of authority, she moved from her seat near the door to kneel at his bedside.

"Look at me, Saviya!"

She raised her face to his and the Marquis saw that her eyes were very wide and a little afraid.

"I love you!" he said. "Do you not understand, my darling, how much I love you?"

"I love you too!" Saviya answered, "but because you are so important . . . of such consequence in the . . . Social World . . . an association with a Gypsy will shock and perhaps disgust your friends."

"If it does, then they are not my friends," the Marquis said, "and besides does anything matter but ourselves? We do not want the gay life in London, Saviya. We can stay here at Ruckley or go abroad for part of the year. I have a yacht that will carry us along the coast of France to anywhere that you fancy. To me it will not matter where as long as we are together."

She drew a deep breath and he knew that she was deeply moved.

Then she said on a sudden note of despair:

"You do not understand!"

"What do I not understand?" he asked gently.

"That you cannot set aside the prejudices, the beliefs, the hatreds of centuries," she answered. "We are, as you say, two people who love each other, but there is a great gulf between us and nothing you can say or do can bridge it."

"That is ridiculous!" the Marquis said sharply. "There is one thing that can bridge it, Saviya, one thing which is stronger than any of the things you have mentioned."

"What is that?" she asked wonderingly.

"Love!" he replied.

As the Marquis spoke he put out his arms and pulled her close against him.

He was sitting up against his pillows and she did not resist him. Her head fell back against his shoulder, and now she was half-sitting, half-lying on the bed.

"Could anything in the world be more important than this?" he asked and then his lips were on hers.

He kissed her fiercely and with a passion which he had been too weak to feel for the past two weeks, but he knew as his mouth took possession of hers that his desire was like a fiery flame burning through his whole body.

Yet at the same time he worshipped with what was almost a reverence the gentleness and sweetness of her.

"I love you!" he said. "Believe me when I tell you, Saviya, there is nothing else in my life except my love for you."

He kissed her again until she trembled and quivered in his arms and then he asked:

"Shall we go away together now and forget that I have any other existence except that I belong to you? Let Jethro be Marquis of Ruckley and own the Estate and everything else. All I want is you and your love."

Saviya put her arms around his neck and now as her lips responded to his he could feel her heart beating against his breast.

Then, when it seemed they had reached the very peak of ecstasy and human nature must break under the strain, very gently Saviya drew herself from his arms.

"I love you," she whispered, "but you must still rest."

The Marquis protested but she put her finger-tips against his lips.

"Rest," she said. "You are tired, and this is not a moment to make decisions."

"Tell me one thing," the Marquis said, "that you

love me as I love you. Tell me, Saviya! I have to hear it as well as know it when I touch you."

"I love you!" she whispered.

Yet there was somehow almost a note of despair in her voice.

Chapter Six

"I'll be going now, M'Lord if there's nothing else Your Lordship requires?" Hobley said.

The Marquis looked up at his Valet from where he was sitting outside the caravan in the shade of the trees.

"Nothing, thank you, Hobley," he said, "but do not forget to ascertain if Colonel Spencer, the Chief Constable, will be at home tomorrow."

"I'll do that, M'Lord."

"Without arousing suspicion," the Marquis admonished. "I do not want anyone to be aware that I am alive until I confront Mr. Jethro."

"I've got it quite clear in my mind, M'Lord," Hobley said with just a touch of rebuke in his voice that the Marquis had thought it necessary to repeat himself.

"Then good-bye, Hobley, and thank you."

"Good-day, M'Lord."

Picking up the empty basket in which he had brought food from the house, Hobley moved between the trees and almost immediately was lost to sight.

It was certainly, the Marquis thought, a perfect place for concealment.

The caravan, with its wooden sides painted in gay colours, was completely hidden by trailing-ivy, shrubs and long strands of convolvulus so that it blended in with the branches of the trees and was, as Saviya had told him, almost invisible.

119

The trees themselves were very thick in this part of the wood. The Marquis wondered if he had ever actually been there before, and decided if he had, he did not remember it.

It was now three weeks since he had been thrown from his horse and stabbed by Jethro's men.

His wound had healed, his collar-bone had knit and he was in fact, as he had protested for some days now, in perfect health.

At the same time his brave words a week earlier that he wished to rise from his bed and confront his cousin had proved too optimistic.

He had no idea how weak he was until when, for the first time, he was on his feet again and could step from the caravan into the wood.

"I am ashamed of being such a weakling," he said to Saviya.

"You ran a very high fever and you also lost a lot of blood."

"I still expected to feel more like a man than a child," the Marquis averred.

"You must be strong to face what lies ahead," Saviya said in a low voice, and the Marquis knew she was still afraid.

"I expect you to give me courage," he said, "and not go on molly-coddling me as you and Hobley have been doing these past weeks."

Nevertheless, after his first sortie into the open air, the Marquis found he was glad to creep back into bed to fall asleep as soon as his head touched the pillow.

Yet every day he had grown stronger and could do more.

Saviya took him for walks through the woods, and he learnt much that he had never known before about the birds and the animals they saw and also the flowers.

She told him strange legends that were connected with Gypsy lore.

About the squirrels—the *romen morga,* or Gyspy

Cats, who are a lucky mascot and particularly effective in the realms of love.

"But the weasel brings ill-luck," Saviya said. "If by chance a Gypsy should kill a weasel the whole tribe will be unfortunate for a long time."

"Superstition about the weasel is very ancient," the Marquis remarked. "It existed in Ancient Greece."

Saviya described how the Gypsies in the Balkans captured young bear-cubs and trained them so that they could dance to amuse the peasants in the villages.

She related that there were groups of Gypsies who were hunters, and who, apart from their skill, had a deep knowledge of the magic rites associated with hunting.

"The Balkan Gypsies," she went on, "will never allow a woman in any circumstances to go near the hunters before they depart in search of game."

One thing Saviya told the Marquis fascinated him: it was the Gypsies who invented lures for line-fishing.

"They were the first to make artificial baits," she said, "such as little wooden fish decorated with tufts of coloured feathers, in the middle of which hooks are hidden."

"I had no idea of that!" the Marquis exclaimed.

"And my father told me it was the Gypsies in Britain," Saviya went on, "who invented the artificial fly for trout fishing."

She looked at him from under her eye-lashes and said with a smile:

"You will doubtless think it un-sporting, but they know how to make magical bait!"

"How do they do that?" the Marquis enquired.

"They are generally made with the gums of resinous plants whose attraction for fish was known centuries ago in Persia," she replied. "But there is another way of coating stones with sweet-smelling oils."

Most of all the Marquis wanted to learn about the Gypsy's proficiency with horses.

"We never say, 'I hope you will live happily,'"
Saviya told him, "but, 'May your horses live long!'"

"All Nomads have revered the horse," the Marquis
remarked. "The Great Khan of the Mongols had a
postal service of three hundred horses."

"Gypsies are strictly forbidden to eat horseflesh,"
Saviya went on, "as they believe it will send them
mad. The Gypsy tribe of Zyghes saddle the horse of
a dead man for three days after he is buried and lead
it to the Grave."

"What happens then?" the Marquis enquired.

"The man who leads the horse calls the owner three
times by name and asks him to dine."

"I believe the Gypsies excel in being able to pass
off an old horse at a Fair by making him appear
young and spritely," the Marquis remarked with a
twinkle in his eyes.

Saviya laughed.

"That is true, and among some tribes there is a
great deal of Magic connected with the trading in
horses."

"And love?" the Marquis questioned. "Is magic necessary to love?"

"Many Gypsies think so," Saviya answered, "but to
me love . . . is magic."

"And to me, my darling," the Marquis told her.

It seemed to the Marquis as they walked together
or sat outside the caravan that Saviya's knowledge
was inexhaustible, and every moment they were together he found her more and more fascinating.

The food she cooked for him, even though Hobley
brought most of it from the House, was different from
anything he had tasted before. Berries, mushrooms,
herbs, nettles, and wild vegetables were all part of
the soups and stews she made over a fire in the pot
that was supported from a tripod of sticks.

"Why does what you cook taste far more delicious
than the food prepared by my extremely expensive
and renowned Chef?" the Marquis enquired.

"I think one reason is that the herbs which I add to

the meat or the chickens that Hobley brings, are fresh," Saviya replied. "Everything you have eaten today I picked this morning."

"It certainly tastes different," the Marquis said appreciatively.

"The Gypsies use few spices and very little salt," Saviya told him. "In fact the only condiment we like is wild garlic."

Sometimes the Marquis felt he was almost like a child asking for "another story." He found an inexpressible delight not only to listen to what Saviya told him, but also to watch her as she talked.

'It is not only her beauty,' he thought.

But it was impossible not to realise that because she was in love she was more beautiful than she had ever been.

Also the strength of her character and her personality shone like a spiritual light and made him feel at times that there was an aura about her that was not of this world.

In the evening when the Marquis had eaten the supper she had prepared for him and Hobley, having got him ready for bed, had gone home, Saviya would sit beside him and they would look through the open door of the caravan into the mystery of the wood outside.

There would be the rustle of the leaves in the evening breeze; the hoot of an owl; the soft scuffle of some animal through the undergrowth. Otherwise there was an indescribable peace.

"You make me very happy," the Marquis said one evening in his deep voice.

"Do I really?" Saviya asked.

"I have never before known real happiness," the Marquis answered.

He raised her hands to his lips and knew as his mouth touched her skin she quivered with the sudden ecstasy.

"I thought what I wanted in life was to be amused," he went on, "to listen to witty, bright conversation;

123

to be made to laugh; to attend the parties given by
my friends. But now I want only to be alone with
you."

"Perhaps if we were together for too long, you
would be . . . bored," she suggested, a little catch in
her breath.

"You know that is not true!" the Marquis replied.
"Always before, when I have been with a woman
and have not actually been feeling passionate about
her, I have been restless."

He kissed Saviya's hands again before he said:

"I think too I have been afraid of being alone."

"And now?"

"I feel," the Marquis replied, "as if a whole new
world was opening before me; a world of discovery,
not only of people, places and things, but of myself
and you."

Saviya turned sideways to lay her head against his
shoulder.

"You are my world," she whispered.

Then the Marquis had put his arms around her
and held her close.

He knew now, sitting outside the caravan, that
Saviya was worried. He had grown to know only too
well without words what she was feeling and especially when she was perturbed.

She was afraid for the morrow, and what might
happen when he confronted Jethro and threw him
out of the House.

The Marquis on the other hand was filled with a
sense of excitement. He knew that something fierce
and primitive within him wished to do battle with his
cousin and punish him for the attempts he had made
on his life.

"Why are you worrying, my darling?" he asked
Saviya.

She moved from the stool on which she had been
sitting to come and kneel beside his chair.

"I cannot help it," she answered.

"Are you being clairvoyant, or merely human in that you are apprehensive?"

She smiled a little forlornly.

"You know that because I love you so deeply I can no longer see the future where you are concerned, but I can feel that you are in . . . danger. Otherwise my love blinds me and I am no longer a witch, but a . . . woman!"

The Marquis laughed.

"Do not sound so tragic about it," he begged, "that is what I want you to be—a woman! My woman! Now and for all time!"

He rose from the chair as he spoke and drew Saviya to her feet to put his arms around her. Tipping back her head, he looked down into her dark, troubled eyes.

"Trust me," he said, "I know what is best for both of us."

Then he kissed her, and they could not think of anything but the rapture which consumed them both and transported them into a world where there was no treachery, no fear, but only love.

Nevertheless, that night before the Marquis went to bed he held Saviya close to him and knew that she was trembling in his arms, but not because she was afraid.

"This is our last night here together," he said slowly. "But after tomorrow we shall never be apart from each other. As soon as I have rid my House of my disreputable cousin and set my affairs in order, we are going away in my yacht."

Saviya gave a little murmur and hid her face against his shoulder.

"We are going away for the rest of the summer," the Marquis said, "and by the time we come back, all the talk, excitement and gossip about us will be over, and some far more amusing scandal will have taken its place!"

He stroked Saviya's head with a gentle hand, feeling her hair like silk beneath his fingers.

"Whatever people say, they will say it behind our backs," he went on, "and why should that worry us? We will cross the Channel and move slowly along the coast of France. I am going to take you to Spain, Saviya."

His arms tightened around her for a moment and he said:

"Anywhere we go together will be like Paradise, but I want to show you the golden beaches and the magnificent Palaces."

Saviya made no answer but the Marquis knew she was listening.

"I have friends in Spain," he said, "who will welcome you because you are beautiful."

"They will think it strange that you are consorting with a Gypsy," Saviya said in a low voice. "The Spanish Gitanos are very poor. They are treated with contempt and have been persecuted by every succeeding Monarch."

"You have been to Spain?" the Marquis asked.

Saviya shook her head.

"Then it will be somewhere new that we can explore together."

The Marquis felt that Saviya was still uncertain, and he said gently:

"We are starting a new life together, Saviya. The prejudices of the old must not encroach on or overshadow our future."

She slipped her arms round his neck and drew his head down to hers.

"I love you!" she whispered. "I love you so desperately! You know that all I want is your happiness?"

"Which is to be with you," the Marquis replied. "There are so many things for us to do. I want to take you to Greece, to the Islands of the Mediterranean. But what does it matter where we go? You hold my whole happiness in your little hands."

Then he was kissing her again, kissing her until

she could no longer think, only feel that she was a part of him and that there was no gulf between them.

The Marquis would have kept her with him much longer, but Saviya insisted that he must rest because of what he had to do the following day. Finally he gave in to her insistence, climbed into the small caravan and went to bed.

He slept peacefully without dreaming, but with a sense of happiness which lingered with him when he awoke.

Saviya had already lit the fire, before Hobley arrived with fresh eggs, newly baked bread and a pat of golden butter from the Marquis's own dairy.

He helped the Marquis to dress while Saviya cooked the eggs and brewed the coffee.

As the Marquis came down the steps of the caravan he saw there was a faint flush on her cheeks from the heat of the fire. In her pretty Gypsy clothes, she looked like the heroine of a theatrical melodrama and far too glamorous to be practical.

Yet the eggs were cooked perfectly and, because she had added a few special herbs to the dish, the Marquis thought it tasted better than any breakfast he had ever eaten at Ruckley House.

"Tell me, Hobley," he said as Saviya poured him a second cup of coffee, "has Mr. Jethro any plans for this morning?"

"I ascertained, M'Lord, that he is rising late," Hobley replied.

"Was he drinking deep last night?" the Marquis enquired.

"He was, M'Lord. Two of his friends left after midnight and a third was posting back to London the very moment that I myself left the House."

"Then Mr. Jethro will be alone?"

"Yes, M'Lord."

"That is what I wanted to know," the Marquis said. "You have ordered the horses?"

"They followed me here," Hobley said. "I left them

127

about fifty yards away, M'Lord. I thought it best for
the grooms not to see the caravan."

"Quite right," the Marquis approved. "And now,
Hobley—be off with you! Collect the Chief Constable
and bring him to the House. We will meet you there
in an hour. Will that give you enough time?"

"Plenty of time, M'Lord."

Hobley turned to go and then said:

"Good luck, M'Lord! It will be a pleasure to have
you back again."

"Thank you, Hobley."

The Valet disappeared and the Marquis resumed
his breakfast, eating everything that Saviya offered
him with a calmness which bespoke an iron control
over his emotions.

"You will be careful?" she said suddenly, as if they
had been talking instead of eating in silence.

"I will be careful for your sake," the Marquis replied. "But after all, what can Jethro do? He has
announced to the whole world that I am dead and
that you are my murderer . . . When I return very
much alive with you beside me, it will be difficult for
his lies to be treated with anything but contempt."

"All the same, he is like a snake or a rat," Saviya
said. "I do not believe that he will give in so easily."

"I have decided," the Marquis told her, "to give
him a choice. Either I will bring charges against him
for attempted murder, or he leaves the country."

He paused and added:

"I would of course prefer the latter course. It would
be unfortunate from the family point of view that
there should be a scandal, or for anyone who bears
our name to be accused of intent to murder."

"I wish you had taken my advice and asked Charles
Collington to be with us this morning," Saviya
sighed.

"I am not proud of the manner in which my cousin
has behaved," the Marquis answered, "and the fewer
people who know what has occurred, the better."

"I can understand that," Saviya murmured.

128

"There have been few scandals in our family over the centuries, very few. My father and my grandfather were respected here in the county and in the House of Lords where they each played their part. When I die, I hope that men will also speak well of me."

It was only as he said the words that the Marquis saw the expression in Saviya's face and knew perceptively that she was thinking that it would not add to his prestige to associate with her.

He put out his hand and caught her wrist as she turned away.

"Do not look like that, my darling," he said. "My private life is my own and no man shall interfere with it. In public we will be very circumspect."

Even as he spoke he realised how difficult it would be to have Saviya living at Ruckley House without everyone being aware of it.

He knew too that he could never insult her by keeping her as he had kept his previous mistresses, in a small house in the less fashionable part of Mayfair where he could visit her at his convenience.

There were, he knew, very many obstacles ahead, but for the moment he thought it best to take one fence at a time.

When he had disposed of Jethro, then he and Saviya could go abroad, and when they returned in the Autumn, they could face the other problems concerning their association.

He tried to draw Saviya to him but she slipped away.

"You have to get ready," she said. "We must be leaving in a few moments and you must think now of what you have to say to your cousin. But watch him! Please, My Lord, watch him carefully!"

There was a little sob in her voice, but the Marquis ignored it.

"I have said before, you must trust me," he replied. "I have been a soldier, Saviya, and I have learnt never to underestimate the enemy."

The horses that Hobley had brought for them were
the best in the Marquis's stables and as he lifted
Saviya into the saddle he said softly:

"I have always wanted to see you ride."

He knew by the sudden light in her eyes that she
too was excited by the magnificence of the horse-
flesh, and the fact that she held the reins in her
hands.

The two grooms who had brought the horses were
astonished at seeing the Marquis, and when he
greeted them there was no mistaking that they were
sincerely pleased to see that he was, contrary to what
they had believed, alive!

They had their own horses, and as the Marquis
mounted they followed him.

It was, Saviya thought, quite a cavalcade that set
off through the woods to emerge finally into the Park.

Ruckley House was looking exquisite in the sunshine, its red bricks warm against the flashing
diamond-paned windows, the curling chimney stacks
silhouetted against the blue sky.

As Saviya raised her eyes to the gabled roofs of
Ruckley House, she saw that the flag was flying.

The Marquis saw it too. His lips tightened and his
eyes were angry.

It was only when the owner was in residence that
the flag flew from the mast on top of the house. That
Jethro had ordered it to be flown indicated that he
already considered himself · the new Marquis of
Ruckley.

They moved across the Park, scattering the deer
who were clustered under the trees, and moved without undue haste towards the court-yard in front of the
main entrance.

'Never,' the Marquis thought, 'has my house looked
more beautiful.'

The lilacs had come into bloom since he had last
seen it, purple and white; their blossoms as lovely as
the showers of golden laburnum and the pink and
white petals of the almond trees.

The daffodils were over, but now the rhododendrons were crimson, pink and purple beside the sweet-smelling yellow azaleas.

'It is worth fighting for,' the Marquis thought to himself.

He knew he would struggle with every breath in his body to prevent Jethro and his dissolute, drunken friends from ruining the peace and beauty that was Ruckley.

Saviya was looking over her shoulder as they drew their horses to a standstill outside the front door.

"There is no sign of Hobley," she said. "We must wait for him."

"I am waiting for no-one," the Marquis replied, and there was a note in his voice which told her he was very angry.

It was as if seeing the house again had brought home to him all too forcefully what he might have lost. Now the calmness with which he had started the day had changed to a deep fury.

He dismounted, and lifted Saviya to the ground.

She wanted to beg him to wait a little longer for the Chief Constable. But knowing that nothing she could say would make any difference, she moved silently beside the Marquis as he strode up the steps towards the front door.

It was opened immediately and, while the footmen in their livery stared in astonishment, Bush gave an exclamation of joy.

"Your Lordship! You are alive!"

"Very much alive!" the Marquis replied.

"We were all sure, quite sure, M'Lord, that you could not have died as they said, but we were afraid, sore afraid when you did not return."

"I am back," the Marquis said. "Where is Mr. Jethro?"

"In the Salon, M'Lord. He has just finished breakfast."

The Marquis strode across the Hall and Saviya followed him.

131

A footman hurried to open the door of the Salon.

Jethro was standing at the far end of the room in front of the fireplace and the expression on his face made Saviya tremble.

He looked exactly as she had seen him the first time, when she had read the Marquis's fortune and known that he was in danger.

Dark-haired, with a long nose, Jethro Ruck could have been good-looking had it not been for his dissolute way of life and an expression on his face which was so shifty, so sinister, that it made people instinctively shrink from contact with him.

His eyes, under heavy eyebrows, were too close together, but it was his mouth, twisted and cynical and perpetually sneering which made him appear so intolerable.

"So you have returned!" he said in a harsh voice before the Marquis could speak. "I saw you coming across the Park and I am therefore ready to welcome you, dear cousin."

The Marquis advanced further into the room.

"How dare you behave in such a manner!" he said slowly his voice completely under control. "Three times you have tried to kill me, Jethro, and three times you have failed. Now I have had enough!"

"You were born under a lucky star," Jethro Ruck replied and somehow he made it an insult. "Any other man would have died as you should have done by the accidents I contrived, but you have survived."

"Yes, I have survived," the Marquis said, "and now we will have no more of them."

"So you think to prevent me inheriting?" Jethro Ruck asked. "But I am not defeated, Cousin Fabius —not yet!"

"I am afraid your plots, ingenious though they may be," the Marquis said scathingly, "have become too insupportable for me to tolerate them any longer. I therefore intend, Jethro, to give you an ultimatum."

His cousin laughed and it was an unpleasant sound.

"And what are you suggesting?" he jeered. "That

you hang me from a gibbet or incarcerate me in the dungeons?"

"Neither," the Marquis said. "You will either stand trial for attempted murder and perjury, or you will go into self-imposed exile on the Continent. I will support you generously, Jethro, so long as you never again set foot in England."

Again Jethro Ruck laughed.

"Well thought out, Fabius!" he said, "a typical 'gentleman's compromise.' You hope I will choose the latter course because it will involve no scandal for the family."

"For once we are in agreement," the Marquis said.

"And do you really think," Jethro Ruck asked, and now his voice was smooth and silky and all the more sinister, "that I intend to go abroad and leave you in possession here with your Gypsy mistress?"

The Marquis stiffened.

"You will leave Saviya's name out of our discussions, Jethro," he said sharply. "You have defamed her enough already."

"You really imagine that I, a Ruck, could defame a Gypsy?"

"I have already said," the Marquis remarked, "we will not discuss Saviya. Let us concern ourselves with your movements."

Saviya was watching Jethro Ruck, and she realised that as he stood almost as if he was at attention facing the Marquis, with his hands behind his back, he had a kind of courage that was a part of his heritage.

She had known that he would not bow to circumstances; that he would not acknowledge defeat; that he would fight, even as the Marquis would fight, to the last ditch.

Vile and wicked though Jethro might be, there was good blood in his veins and whatever happened, he was no coward.

"I want your answer," the Marquis insisted.

Now there was steel in his tone as if he was coming to the end of his patience.

133

"I will give you my answer," Jethro Ruck replied, "and I will give it very clearly, Cousin Fabius, so that there will be no mistake. You have always despised me. You have always looked down at me, you have always believed I was of little consequence, but now, at last, I have the whip hand!"

The Marquis merely raised his eye-brows to show he did not understand what his cousin was saying, and Jethro Ruck went on:

"You are going to die, Fabius, as I have meant you to do all along. It is better that it should be at this moment, because it will appear, at least to the world, as honourable and in the family tradition."

"I do not know what you are talking about," the Marquis said. "Stop this nonsense and answer my question. Will you face a trial or go abroad."

"I will do neither!" Jethro Ruck retorted. "I stay here and enjoy myself as the sixth Marquis of Ruckley."

As he spoke, he drew his hands from behind his back and Saviya gave a little gasp of horror.

Jethro Ruck held two pistols and each was pointing at the Marquis's chest.

"If you kill me," the Marquis said contemptuously, "you will be hanged for murder."

"On the contrary," Jethro Ruck replied, "I shall have killed you in self-defence."

He gave a little chuckle.

"You have played right into my hands, dear Fabius. The servants saw you arrive and they will all be prepared to swear that you were in a vengeful mood as you strode up the steps and crossed the Hall. They will have heard us talking, and what could be more understandable than that you should lose your temper at my impertinence and shoot me down with your own dueling-pistol?"

There was so much venom in his voice that Saviya felt as if she could not move and that her breath was constricted in her throat.

She saw now how mad they had been to come to

the house without weapons; without any defence against a man more deadly than a cobra; more vengeful than a cornered rat.

"You are thinking," Jethro Ruck said jeeringly, "that your Gypsy strumpet might give evidence against me. Do not blind yourself to the truth. No-one would take the word of a Gypsy against that of the sixth Marquis of Ruckley!"

There was a note of triumph in his tone before he went on:

"You have threatened me, Fabius. No-one can deny that. Unfortunately you have not provided yourself with the means to make your threat effective. My plan, therefore, is quite clear."

He smiled the smile of a man who holds all the trump cards.

"As I will tell the Magistrates, you threatened me, Fabius and, when I would not agree to your preposterous suggestions, you attempted to kill me. This pistol, which has been fired, will be found in your hand. To protect myself, I returned your fire and, being of course a better shot than you, I am the victor!"

There was something horrible and gloating in the way Jethro Ruck spoke.

Then as he raised the pistol in his right hand slowly to bring it down at the Marquis, there was a sudden movement!

Even as his finger tightened on the trigger, a flash of steel shot through the air and entered his throat.

It was so quick that the Marquis could hardly understand what had happened.

Jethro Ruck staggered and then fell backwards. As he did so, there was a deafening report and the bullet from his pistol shattered the ceiling above their heads.

For a moment the Marquis stood shocked and unable to move. And before he could do so there was a voice behind him and footsteps crossing the room.

The Marquis turned his head.

"Colonel Spencer!" he ejaculated.

"I am glad to see you are unharmed, Fabius."

The Chief Constable was an elderly but distinguished figure, and his expression was one of gravity.

"You heard what was said?" the Marquis enquired.

"I was trying to make up my mind what I should do," Colonel Spencer replied. "I had the feeling that if I entered the room unexpectedly Jethro might have finished you off quicker than he intended."

"I threw the dagger which killed him," the Marquis said quickly, putting his hand as he spoke on Saviya's to prevent her from contradicting him.

"It was an act of self-defence," the Chief Constable said as if he understood, "and it is quite immaterial who handled the weapon in question."

"Thank you, Colonel," the Marquis said gratefully. "I would not have wished my—future wife to be involved in this unpleasantness."

As he spoke, he felt Saviya's fingers go rigid beneath his.

"I will congratulate you, Fabius, under more pleasant circumstances," the Chief Constable said. "At the moment I have my duty to perform."

"I understand," the Marquis said. "Do you wish me to send for the servants?"

The Chief Constable walked to Jethro Ruck's fallen body and looked down at him.

There was no doubt that he was dead. Blood was oozing from the wound and there was a stream of blood from between his thin lips.

Looking at the dagger, the Marquis knew that it had been a brilliant throw on Saviya's part. She had pierced Jethro's throat in exactly the most vulnerable spot, and with a force which he knew came from the flexibility of the muscles in her wrist.

"I am sorry your cousin's life should have ended like this," the Chief Constable said quietly. "I have known you both since you were children, and as you grew up together you appeared to be close friends."

"We were," the Marquis answered, "until when we

became men, Jethro was eaten up with jealousy and envy. He wanted so desperately to be in my shoes."

"Hobley has told me," the Chief Constable said, "of the other attempts he made on your life."

"Because you were my father's friend, Colonel," the Marquis said in a low voice, "can you arrange that there is as little scandal as possible?"

"I will do what I can," the Colonel promised. "As I was actually present at Jethro's death, my evidence will be sufficient for the Magistrates. It was a duel of honour and there will be few legal formalities."

"In a duel of honour it is customary for the survivor to go abroad for a few months, and that is what I intend to do," the Marquis answered.

"That is wise of you," the Colonel approved, "and now I suggest you leave everything in my hands, Fabius. As a very great friend of the Ruck family, I promise you that the real truth of what has happened between you and Jethro will never go beyond the four walls of this room."

"Thank you, Colonel," the Marquis said. "I knew I could rely on you, and that you of all people would understand."

He held out his hand and then as they shook hands the Chief Constable said:

"I want above all things, Fabius, to see you take your father's place in the County. I know that a young man who has played a brilliant part in the war needs the relaxation and amusements that only London can give him. But there is work to be done here."

His eyes were on the Marquis's face and he continued:

"With the new lands, which I hear have come into your possession, I hope that Ruckley House will see a great deal more of you in the future."

The Marquis knew that what the Chief Constable was saying to him had a far deeper meaning than appeared on the surface.

He was well aware that without mentioning Saviya she was uppermost in Colonel Spencer's mind.

The Marquis had recognised as Jethro staggered and died from the impact of the dagger that there was only one place for Saviya in his life—and that was as his wife.

She had not only saved his life for the third time, but she had killed a man in his defence.

As he thought of her he realised she was not at his side. He looked round the room, then thought that perhaps, to avoid looking at the dead body of Jethro, she had gone in search of The Reverend.

The Chief Constable had already moved towards the door, and as the Marquis followed him into the Hall he started to give instructions to Bush for the removal of Jethro Ruck's body.

The Marquis began to walk towards the Library. Then as he passed a footman, he said:

"Where is Miss Saviya?"

"She left the house, M'Lord."

The Marquis looked at the man in astonishment and then he strode across the Hall and out onto the steps.

The Chief Constable's carriage was outside and Hobley was talking to the Coachman.

The Valet came towards the Marquis with a question in his eyes.

"Where is Miss Saviya?" the Marquis asked for the second time.

"She came out a few moments ago, M'Lord, and took the horse on which I returned with Colonel Spencer, and rode towards the wood."

"Fetch me a horse from the stables," the Marquis said sharply to a footman who was standing behind him.

The man ran off and Hobley looking up at his master found it impossible to ask the questions which hovered on his lips.

He knew that something had gravely perturbed the Marquis and, with an anxious expression on his face, he went into the house to find out for himself what had happened.

There was a few minute's delay before a groom appeared from the stables riding the Marquis's favourite black stallion.

He jumped down and almost before he reached the ground, the Marquis had swung himself into the saddle.

Without a word he galloped off across the Park towards the woods.

As he went he was afraid with a fear that was almost like an iron hand clutching at his heart.

Chapter Seven

The Marquis urged his horse on until he reached the woods, wondering how he could find Saviya's tribe and where they were likely to be.

He remembered she had told him that they had moved, after Jethro began searching for her.

While the Marquis realised that it was impossible to hide fifty people for long, the woods were large enough for him to have to spend several days in searching for them unless he was exceptionally lucky.

He had the inescapable feeling that Saviya had always meant to leave him when he was well enough.

He knew she was deeply conscious of the differences of rank between them, and she was far too intelligent not to realise, as he did, the unavoidable implications were he to set up a lasting liaison with a Gypsy.

Saviya was so sensitive, and they were so closely attuned to each other, that the Marquis knew she was well aware of his anxiety concerning the problems which would arise from their living together. And marriage would arouse even greater difficulties, not only from his point of view, but from Saviya's.

He knew she had not spoken idly when she had said that the most terrible thing that could happen to a Gypsy was to be exiled from the tribe.

Because their society was so close-knit and they kept themselves apart from other people, exile was to them as bad if not worse than excommunication to a Roman Catholic.

Marriage between a Gypsy and a non-Gypsy was universally disapproved by all the tribes that were pure Romany.

Saviya had told the Marquis once that, even though in some exceptional instances a marriage might not bring exclusion from the tribe, the outlaw whether it was a man or woman no longer had the right to the name of Gypsy.

"Sometimes," she went on, "this ostracism extends to the whole family and lineage of the guilty party."

"That sounds to me unfair—cruel!" the Marquis exclaimed.

"It is worse than death!" Saviya had said quietly.

Remembering this conversation now, the Marquis was certain that the fact that he had told the Chief Constable that Saviya was to be his wife had driven her away from him.

"I love you!" he had said to Saviya one evening when she had been sitting in the caravan at the door, and he had been watching her from the bed.

He saw the sudden light in her eyes which illuminated her face and made her almost dazzlingly beautiful.

Then he had asked:

"What is love, Saviya? For I have never known it until now."

She had looked away from him and he knew by the sudden concentration in her face that she was trying to find a serious and sensible answer to his question.

"I think that love," she said after a moment, "is when someone else matters so completely that one no longer has even a thought of self. One almost ceases to exist because only in the other is one alive."

She turned her face towards the Marquis and her eyes shone like stars as she finished:

"One lives for him and one would . . . die for him."

"Is that how you feel about me?" the Marquis asked.

She had risen then to come and kneel beside his bed.

"You know it is. All I want is for you to be happy."

"I am happy as long as you are with me."

He had held her close and yet with a new perception he knew that she was not entirely his.

There was some barrier between them; some reserve that he had felt and not understood. Yet now, he thought with a sense of despair, he knew what it was.

'How can I convince her,' he asked himself, 'that nothing is of importance except our love, except the need we have for each other?'

He remembered how in the past he had never believed that he could fall in love. He had not understood when Eurydice had told him that love was more important than rank.

She had given up being a Duchess for an American whose way of life was entirely different from her own, and with whom she could in fact have little in common except love.

No! He had not understood.

He had even been inclined to laugh at anyone who could be swept off their feet to such an extent that they would alter their whole way of life—forget the past and all it implied for an emotion so intangible that one could not even explain it.

'I am not laughing now!' the Marquis told himself almost savagely.

He had to find Saviya, but he knew that the sands of time were running out.

If, as he suspected, the Gypsies were in the process of leaving, if they once moved away from the vicinity, how would he ever find her again?

They were wanderers and nomads. At the same time centuries of being persecuted had taught them how to evade detection; how to vanish into a labyrinth of woods and mountains, hills and valleys, so that it was almost impossible to find them.

The Marquis, riding as quickly as he could, guided

his horse through the tree-trunks until he came to the place in the wood where he himself had been hidden for three weeks.

With a sudden pang of dismay he realised the caravan was no longer there.

Saviya's own special painted caravan, in which he had known a happiness that had never been his before, was not where he had left it that morning.

Then he told himself that if it had so recently been moved, there should be the marks of the wheels.

His eyes searched the ground but it was not easy. There was either moss on which no marks could be seen or low undergrowth through which the wheels of a cart could pass without leaving an impression.

Twisting and turning, straining his eyes for some clue which might lead him to Saviya, the Marquis had ridden for over half an hour before finally he came to an open space.

He knew immediately that this was where the camp must have been before Jethro had tried to kill him, and Saviya had saved his life. There were the remains of fires but they were only ashes.

It was not a camp-site that had just been vacated, but one on which the woodland flowers were already beginning to hide the fact that it had ever been used by human beings.

But here at last the Marquis had the clue! A wheel mark!

He could see that it would lead him deeper into the forest that stood on the south side of the Estate and was in parts almost impenetrable.

'That is exactly where the Gypsies would have gone if they wished to hide,' he told himself.

He found what appeared to be a bridle-path and knew it was just wide enough to allow a caravan to travel along it.

He followed it, all the time conscious that he must move quickly or Saviya might elude him forever.

He knew then with a pain that was both physical and mental that he could not lose her.

It was not only her beauty that attracted him. It was that she was in all truth the other part of himself.

He knew now why he had always felt lonely in his life and somehow apart from other people. He had not been a whole person—he had not been complete. It was Saviya who was the completion of himself as he was the completion of her.

'I love you!' he said in his heart. 'Oh, my darling, do you not understand how much I love you? How could you do this to me?'

He rode on feeling at times almost frantic as the wood bewildered him, and he felt as if instead of advancing he was going round in circles and coming back to the place from which he had first started.

Then suddenly—so suddenly it was almost a shock —he found them!

There were eight caravans, most of them far larger and more elaborate than Saviya's, and they were on the point, the Marquis knew, of moving off.

The horses were between the shafts, some of the Gypsies were already holding the reins in their hands, others were folding tents and stowing a number of objects away inside and beneath the caravans.

They were talking amongst themselves in their own language, until as the Marquis appeared there was a sudden silence.

He reined in his horse and a number of dark-skinned faces were turned towards him and suspicious black eyes regarded him questioningly.

They were an exceedingly good-looking collection of people, the Marquis appreciated, with their high cheek-bones, black eyes and dark hair. They were in fact more Russian-looking than any Gypsies he had seen in the past.

There were children with small, oval faces and large gazelle-like eyes, and several older women with red handkerchiefs over their heads and huge gold ear-rings dangling from their ears.

The Marquis moved his horse forward a little.

"I wish," he said, "to speak to your *Voivode*."

The man to whom he addressed his remark did not answer but merely pointed his hand to the far end of the clearing.

As the Marquis rode in the direction he saw a rather more elaborate caravan than the rest and standing in front of it, apparently unaware of his approach, was a tall man talking with Saviya.

The man saw him first and Saviya turned. The Marquis saw a sudden expression of radiant gladness on her face. Then it disappeared as if a cloud hid the sun.

The Marquis rode up to them and dismounted.

He found the *Voivode* was almost as tall as himself, and anyone would have known by his bearing and his clothes that he was a Chieftain.

His coat was blue and he wore very high boots. On his short jacket he had a large number of gold buttons and there was a heavy gold chain hung with pendants round his neck.

The Marquis had heard Saviya speak of the Voivode's staff called *bare esti robli rupui*, which was the last remaining relic of a King's sceptre.

It was made entirely of silver and the hilt, octagonal in shape, was adorned with a red tassel. The staff was engraved with the *Semno*, the authentic 'Sign' of the Gypsies comprising the five ritual figures.

The Marquis held out his hand.

"I am the Marquis of Ruckley and you, I think, are Saviya's father."

"I have been expecting you," the Voivode replied.

"And yet you were leaving?" the Marquis said sharply.

He looked at Saviya as he spoke and saw in her eyes raised to his a look of pleading as if she wanted him to understand why she had run away from him.

"What do you want with us?" the Voivode asked. "We are grateful for the hospitality of your woods. Now it is time for us to go."

"I have come," the Marquis said quietly, "to ask

your permission to take your daughter, Saviya, as my wife."

"You would marry her?"

There was no surprise in the Voivode's voice. He merely looked at the Marquis as if he was seeking deep into his character and personality to find the answer to his question.

He had a dignity about him which made it not an impertinent act, but simply the summing up of one man by another without a question of class or caste.

"No!" Saviya said before her father could speak. "No, it is not . . . possible!"

Her voice was passionate with intensity.

Then sharply, and in a voice of authority, the Voivode spoke to her in Romany.

The Marquis could not understand the words but the sense was very obvious.

He was rebuking her, telling her it was not her place to speak. Saviya bent her head.

"I am sorry, father," she said in English.

"We will discuss this," the Voivode said to the Marquis, "and Saviya, I wish you to hear what I have to say."

He stepped past the Marquis as he spoke to address the tribe.

He obviously told them they would not be leaving for a little while; for the Gypsy men, who had been watching with undisguised curiosity the Marquis's conversation with the Voivode, now turned away to unharness their horses.

The women began to re-kindle the fire in the centre of the clearing, which was practically extinguished.

The Voivode led the way to his caravan and Saviya brought a chair which she set down beside the steps.

The Voivode seated himself on the steps and Saviya sank down on the grass at his feet.

The Marquis tried to meet her eyes; to re-assure her; to tell her by a look if not by words not to be afraid.

But her head was still bowed after her father's rebuke and her eyes were on the grass.

She looked very lovely but sadly forlorn, and the Marquis longed to put his arms around her and hold her close.

He knew she was unhappy. At the same time she had been unable to repress the sudden radiance in her eyes when she had first seen him riding towards them.

A Gypsy approached the Voivode and the Marquis was offered a glass of wine which he accepted.

It was red and a good quality. He supposed that the Gypsies must have brought it with them on their journey across Europe.

The horses were unharnessed and taken away from the caravan, and now that they were out of earshot of the other members of the tribe the Voivode said with a grave voice:

"You wish to marry Saviya?"

"I want her to be my wife," the Marquis replied.

He saw a little quiver go through Saviya as he spoke, but still she did not raise her head.

"This is what I knew was Saviya's destiny," the Voivode said slowly.

The Marquis looked at him in considerable surprise. Such a reply was far from what he had expected.

The Voivode was a handsome man of about fifty. His face was very thin, his cheek-bones prominent, but he must, the Marquis thought, have been exceedingly handsome in his youth. Even then he would have had an air of authority about him; a man born to lead, perhaps to rule.

"Saviya will have explained to you," the Voivode went on, "that the Kalderash are not only smiths but also have a knowledge of magic. It was this knowledge which guided me here."

"You mean," the Marquis asked, "that you knew by clairvoyance that Saviya would meet me and that we would fall in love with each other?"

"That is a simple way of putting it," the Voivode agreed.

Although his English was good he spoke with a very pronounced accent.

"Then I have your permission?" the Marquis insisted.

"There is something I have to say to you first," the Voivode said, "something which I intended to tell Saviya when she wished to marry."

Saviya raised her head. The Marquis saw there was a look of surprise in her face.

"You do not know anything about our race," the Voivode went on speaking to the Marquis, "but you must have learnt from Saviya that no Gypsy girl would ordinarily have been allowed to behave as she has behaved these past weeks; coming first to your house to read your books, and then being constantly in your company."

"I did not understand it, father," Saviya said.

"You were permitted such behaviour," the Voivode explained, "because I knew that this, Saviya, was your only chance of finding yourself a husband— otherwise you would have remained un-wed!"

Saviya was puzzled.

"But why?"

"Because I could not have sanctioned your marriage to any member of our tribe or to any Romany," the Voivode replied.

Saviya looked utterly bewildered. The Marquis with his eyes on the Voivode's face was listening intently.

"I have a story to tell you," the Voivode said.

It was obvious as he began to speak that he had a command of words which the Marquis would not have expected from a Gypsy, even a tribal Chief.

Perhaps it was his Hungarian blood which made him not only eloquent but able to speak with the culture of a man who had lived a very different life from the majority of Gypsies.

It was true also there was magic in the way he made the story seem so real.

Zindelo was the son of the *Voivode* of the Kalder-ash in Hungary, and their particular tribe was under the patronage of one of the great Hungarian nobles. Their music gave them a special prestige and they were widely respected.

They were rich; they were accepted as part of the community; and Zindelo was acknowledged one of the most attractive young men that could be found anywhere in the country.

Great ladies smiled on him, but he was exceedingly proud of his Romany blood and he would not seek love outside his tribe.

Nevertheless, at twenty-one he had not found any girl whom he wished to marry and had refused all suggestions from his father that he should settle down.

It was then the Hungarian nobleman, on whose ground they were encamped, was sent by the Tsar of Russia some dancers from St. Petersburg for his private theatre.

A great fête was arranged for their entertainment, and when they arrived Society from all over Hungary gathered to see them dance.

The majority of the dancers were from the Imperial Ballet, but the Tsar had included a number of Gypsy dancers and singers who were widely famed in Russia.

Among them was a young dancer called Tekla with whom young Zindelo fell in love the moment he saw her, and she with him.

They were married and she did not return to St. Petersburg. The tribe wandered around Hungary, Rumania and into Austria, for there was much that Zindelo, now the Voivode, wished to show his bride.

It was when they were in Germany and had suffered some minor attempts at persecution that Zindelo decided they should visit Britain.

They went to the coast and found a ship that was sailing for Aberdeen.

Some thirty of the tribe, mostly young and adventurous like Zindelo himself, decided they would like to visit Scotland and then trek south through England and back to the Continent.

It seemed a great adventure, but unfortunately the passage was very rough.

By this time Zindelo and Tekla had been married for nearly three years and a child born before they left Hungary had now reached the age of fifteen months.

Gypsy children are proverbially strong, but the baby Saviya sickened during the voyage, as did her mother.

The ship nearly foundered, and while Zindelo was exhilarated by the storm, he realised that his wife, never having been to sea before, was distraught not only by her own sea-sickness but with worry for her child.

By the time they reached Aberdeen, Tekla was in a state of collapse.

Highly-strung, her Russian blood made her more prone to melancholy and depression than the other women, and by the time they set foot on Scottish soil, he was desperately worried about his wife and his child.

The baby had refused to eat or drink during the whole of the voyage and was now emaciated and very weak.

Tekla was hysterical with anxiety and her own health had suffered to the point that she was running a fever.

They camped not far from the sea. The weather was cold but invigorating, and soon the other members of the tribe began to recover and take an interest in their surroundings.

There was plenty of wild game to be found on the moorland, and hot stews cooked over a peat fire soon had them laughing and singing again.

But Tekla grew worse and the baby weaker.

"I was sitting beside my tent one evening almost in despair," the Voivode recounted, "when one of the tribe came to tell me that a woman wished to speak with me.

"She was standing under the darkness of the trees outside the light thrown by the fire.

"When I reached her I saw that she was elderly with strong features.

" 'There is something I wish to say to you,' she told me, 'But we must not be overheard.'

"We moved a little way into the shadow of the trees.

" 'What is it?' I enquired.

"I thought perhaps she wanted her fortune told. It is the usual reason for which women approach us Gypsies in whatever part of the world we travel.

" 'I have known Gypsies for many years,' she said. 'For all their faults they are kind to their children and good parents. I want you to take this child and bring her up as your own.'

"I had had many strange requests made to me, but this was extraordinary.

" 'I am sorry,' I replied, 'we are Romanies. We do not want other people's children and we do not steal them, despite the stories that are told about us.'

" 'If you do not take this child,' the Scottish woman said, 'it will die!'

" 'Why? What is wrong with it?' I asked.

" 'There is someone who wishes to kill it!'

"I looked at her incredulously.

" 'It is the truth,' she said, seeing the disbelief in my eyes. 'This child belongs to a nobleman but the poor bairn's mother died in child-birth and her father has married again.'

"She spoke with such sincerity," the Voivode explained, "that I knew she was telling me the truth.

" 'And who wishes to kill the child?' I enquired.

" 'The Master re-married. She was determined to get him almost before my poor mistress was cold in

152

her grave,' the Scottish woman said with venom in her voice. 'And now she herself has had a premature baby. It is a girl, and she is told she can have no more.'

" 'Is that such a tragedy?' I asked jokingly, 'the world is full of women as it is.'

" 'In Scotland,' came the reply, 'if there is no son, a daughter will inherit—the eldest daughter!'

"I began to see what the woman was trying to tell me.

" 'So you mean,' I enquired almost incredulously, 'your master's new wife intends to kill this child so that her own can be their heir?'

" 'She will kill her, make no mistake of that,' the Scotswoman replied. 'This evening I found her in the Nursery with a pillow in her hands. If I had not come in at that moment, she would have suffocated this poor wee girlee in her cot.'

" 'It is sad—very sad,' I commiserated, 'but I am afraid I can do nothing. If I were to take the child of a Gorgio, people would say it was stolen. Can you imagine the hue and cry there would be?'

" 'Please,' the woman pleaded with me. 'Please, save the bairn's life. I would not have brought her to you had not somebody said to me only yesterday that she is dark enough to be a Gypsy. Take her away with you. Who will notice one more baby in your camp?'

"She pulled the child's shawl away from its face as she spoke. I saw it was very small and had dark hair, thicker than was usual for a child of that age.

"I looked down at it, feeling sorry it must die, and knowing there was nothing I could do about it.

"Then I heard a sudden cry. It came from my tent.

"Turning, I ran away without a word, knowing it was my wife's voice that called me.

"She was sitting up in bed and she was half delirious. I caught her in my arms.

" 'What is the matter? What has upset you?' I asked.

" 'It was a . . . dream,' she cried. 'I dreamt that Saviya was . . . dead! Dead!'

"She seemed to scream the words, and holding her close I reached for a potion of soothing herbs that had been made for her earlier in the day by one of our women.

"She drank it and seemed immediately to grow a little quieter.

" 'It was only a foolish dream, Tekla,' I said. 'Go to sleep.'

" 'You will look after Saviya?' she begged.

" 'I will look after her, I promise. She is asleep. Even the noise you have made has not awakened her.'

"I put my wife down against the pillows, saw her eyes close, and then I looked in the basket on the other side of the caravan where my child was sleeping. She was dead!"

The Marquis saw Saviya had been unable to move while the Voivode was speaking. Her eyes were fixed on his face, and the Marquis felt as if every nerve in his own body was tense for fear he should miss a word of what was being related.

The Voivode went on to say how he picked up his baby daughter in an agony of grief, and as he had done so he wondered how he could tell his wife.

Already she was almost mentally unhinged by the dangers of the voyage and her anxiety over her child.

"I knew then," the Voivode went on, "that Fate had brought me the answer. I returned to the Scottish woman."

"You exchanged the babies!" the Marquis exclaimed.

"The woman changed their clothes," the Voivode replied, "and as she did so she kept repeating how little difference there was between the two children. Both were small and rather under-sized. Both had dark hair.

" 'I told you my bairn looked like a Gypsy,' she

said, when I held the living child in my arms and my little dead daughter was in hers."

"Your wife did not note the difference?" the Marquis asked.

"She was very ill for a long time," the Voivode answered, "and because I thought it was wise we did not linger in Scotland, we set off south immediately."

He drew in his breath as if he remembered how anxious he was to leave Scotland.

"Saviya—the new Saviya—never left my arms, and no-one in the tribe had any idea that she was not the same baby that had crossed the sea with us.

"By the time we were back in Europe, I had almost forgotten myself that there had ever been another child, and that it had died because I had been foolish enough to take my tribe to Scotland instead of remaining in Europe."

"Then I am not your . . . daughter!" Saviya murmured, and there was a little throb in her voice as she said it.

"Not of my blood," the Voivode answered, "but you know that you have always held a part of my heart."

Saviya's face was very pale.

"I cannot . . . believe it!" she cried. "I cannot grasp the fact that I am not a . . . Romany."

"Now you understand," the Voivode told her, "why I could never have allowed you to marry into the tribe. Our blood must remain pure, and even while to save my wife's sanity and your life I adopted you, it would have been against my every instinct to allow you, a Gorgio, to marry one of us."

"You still feel that about . . . me after all these . . . years I have been with . . . you?" Saviya asked.

"You know that it is the code by which we live," the Voivode said simply.

The Marquis did not speak. He wanted to reassure Saviya, but at the same time he knew what a shock this had been to her, and at the moment he was an outsider.

She must grapple alone with something which concerned only herself, because it involved her whole past.

Now the Voivode in a different tone of voice, as if he now set aside past events, said:

"You wish to marry Saviya. Because I cannot insult my tribe by letting them know they have been deceived, I will ask you to marry her according to Gypsy law, and to make this possible I will, if you agree, make you my brother by the exchange of blood."

"I have heard of such a ceremony," the Marquis replied.

"It is not often performed and not universally acceptable," the Voivode said. "But on this occasion, because I must not lose the respect and authority that is mine by right, I shall present you to the tribe. Afterwards you will be married."

He glanced at Saviya with a little smile on his lips before he added:

"Before a wedding there are of course preparations to be made. Go now, My Lord, and return a little later in the day."

"I know it is traditional," the Marquis said slowly, "for the bridegroom not only to give a gift of money to the parents of the bride, but also to contribute to the feast that follows the ceremony. I trust that you will allow me to do both?"

"It is allowed!" the Voivode said with an inclination of his head.

"Then may I suggest that two or three of your tribe wait at the edge of the wood. This will make it possible for my servants to find you," the Marquis said. "And may I also ask that at the time appointed for my return I have an escort. I had great difficulty in finding you."

"It shall be done," the Voivode agreed. "And now while I speak to my people, you may have two minutes speech with Saviya. But not more. It offends our custom!"

He walked away as he spoke and Saviya rose to her feet.

"I cannot . . . believe what my . . . Father has told us," she said miserably. "I am a Gypsy! I have always been a Gypsy!"

"I think we both know that he was speaking the truth," the Marquis said in his deep voice.

He looked down at her white, unhappy face and said very gently:

"Do not be afraid, my darling. Everything will work out for the best! The only thing that really matters is that we have each other."

"Do you still want . . . me?" she whispered with a little catch in her throat.

"Need you really ask me that question?" the Marquis enquired.

She looked into his eyes. It seemed for a moment as though they were close against each other and he held her in his arms.

"I love you!" he said softly. "Remember nothing else except that I love you and tonight you will be my wife."

He raised her hands to his lips, then walked to where his horse was being held by a Gypsy boy. He mounted it.

As he rode away he heard the Voivode calling his people round him, and knew that he was going to tell them that tonight Saviya would marry a Gorgio.

It was nearly six o'clock when the Marquis drove across the Park in his Phaeton.

The Gypsies had shown him a quick way from the camp to where the cart-track made by the Foresters ran into the wood.

The Marquis was dressed as elegantly as if he was about to attend a Reception at Carlton House.

His cravat, intricately tied by Hobley, was snowy white against his chin and a jewelled fob hung from his waist-coat over pantaloons the colour of pale champagne.

He had been extremely busy since he had left the camp in the morning, writing numerous notes which he had dispatched to London by grooms.

One of them was to Charles Collington to tell him that Jethro was dead.

He was well aware that his friend Charles must have been desperately perturbed all the time he had been missing, and he knew that if anyone would be glad to think Jethro no longer threatened him it would be Charles.

There were several other letters the Marquis found urgent. Then he went to the Library to find The Reverend and have a long conversation with him.

He sent to the Gypsy camp an enormous amount of food and several cases of champagne, although he could not help thinking that the Gypsies would prefer the rich red wine to which they were accustomed.

It was with a feeling of almost indescribable happiness that the Marquis drove towards the woods.

He was no longer overshadowed by the problems that lay ahead. He was no longer apprehensive about what the future might hold. All he could think of was Saviya: her beauty, her softness, her sweetness, and her love.

He knew that while many women had loved him in their own way, what they had felt for him had never been the same as the mystical wonder that he saw in Saviya's eyes, or felt in the trembling of her lips when he kissed her.

'I will make her happy!' he told himself.

Then as he reached the shadow of the trees he saw the Gypsies waiting for him.

They were two young men, dark-haired, eloquent-eyed, finely-built and as beautiful in their own way as any Greek God.

They were dressed in a very different manner from the nondescript clothing they were wearing when the Marquis had entered the camp that morning.

Now there were red sashes around their waists and round their heads. There were ear-rings hanging from their ears, and the jewelled hilts of long knives were gleaming in their waistbands.

They led the Marquis's Phaeton a little way into the wood and then invited him to alight.

He knew that they wished him to go the rest of the way on foot so that his groom sitting on the back of the Phaeton could take the horses home and would not therefore be a spectator of anything that was to happen.

The Marquis gave the order. The horses were turned and were driven back the way they had come.

Then, with a Gypsy on either side of him, he walked on through the trees to the camp.

There was a huge fire blazing in the centre of it, and the caravans were drawn round it in a circle, with the exception of Saviya's which stood a little apart from the rest.

This the Marquis saw with a quick glance was decorated with flowers and greenery.

The Gypsies were clustered round the Voivode. He looked even more magnificent in a coat ornamented with gold buttons and a necklace which flashed with jewels. He held his staff in his hand and beside him stood Saviya.

She was wearing a dress not unlike the one in which she had danced for Sir Algernon, but now her head-dress was more like a crown and glittered with jewels set in gold.

There were gems around her neck and at her wrists, and her skirt was richly embroidered. There were coloured ribbons falling on either side of her face almost in the semblance of a veil.

Slowly, the Marquis advanced towards the Voivode while Saviya looked down only at the ground, her head bent.

Earlier in the day the Marquis had sent, as he knew was correct, a small casket filled with gold coins, and he saw that it now stood on a small table behind the Voivode.

As he reached the Voivode the Gypsy cried in a loud voice:

"You have asked that you should marry my daughter who is one of this tribe and a Romany."

"I have requested your permission to do so," the Marquis replied, feeling that was the answer that was expected of him.

"I cannot give my only child to a Gorgio," the Voivode went on, "but are you prepared to become one of us—to become in fact my brother, because my blood is your blood and your blood is mine?"

"I should be honoured," the Marquis answered.

The Voivode obviously repeated in Romany what had been said. Then taking the Marquis's hand in his, he made a small incision on his wrist with a jewelled knife.

When there was a mark of blood, he cut his own, then pressed his wrist against the Marquis's and their blood intermingled.

As he did so the Voivode proclaimed the new relationship between them, saying it was the Marquis's duty to live from then on in accordance with Gypsy Law.

When he had finished, Saviya came nearer, and now she and the Marquis stood facing the Voivode, the Marquis on the right, Saviya on the left, holding hands.

The Voivode spoke some words in Romany and one of the tribe came forward to hand him a bunch of twigs.

"These twigs," the Voivode said to the Marquis, "come from seven different kinds of trees."

Then reverting to Romany, he made an incantation as he snapped the twigs one by one and threw them to the winds.

"This is the meaning of the marriage bond," he said to the Marquis and Saviya, "and it is wrong to break your pledge to one another until either of you have died.

"As man and wife," he went on, "you will have to give and to share. Go Saviya, and fetch bread, salt and water."

Saviya left the Marquis's side and brought back from her caravan a basket with a loaf of bread in it, a small bag of sea salt and an earthenware jar filled with water.

She put down the bread and salt on the table beside the Voivode and, lifting up the earthenware jar, invited the Marquis to drink.

When he had drunk she too drank from the earthenware jar and the Voivode took it from them and smashed it at their feet.

"As many pieces as there are there," he said, "will be the years of your happiness together. Keep one piece each. Preserve it carefully and only if you lose it will misery and loneliness come upon you."

"I will never lose mine, my darling," the Marquis said in a low voice to Saviya.

She looked up at him and he saw there was an expression of ecstasy in her face.

The Voivode again picked up his jewelled knife and took the Marquis's right hand in his. Saviya held out her left hand.

He cut both their wrists just enough so they should bleed, then he held their wrists together so that their blood would mingle and bound them with a silk cord making three knots in it.

"One knot is for constancy," he said, "the second for fertility, and the third for long life."

Then the Voivode cut two pieces of bread from the loaf, sprinkled a little salt on them and handed them to the Marquis and Saviya.

They ate them and when they had done so, the Voivode undid the silk cord which had held their wrists together.

"Keep the cords," he said. "They will remind you that you are tied to each other for all time and you can never be divided."

As he finished speaking, the Gypsies, who had been standing around in silence listening, gave a loud cheer.

Even as their voices rang out the music started—gay, wild music from the violins and the instruments which the Marquis had heard played while Saviya danced.

The Voivode led the bridal couple to the fire where there were a number of cushions and rug-covered seats.

The men all sat down but the women busied themselves with bringing on the feast.

Whatever the Marquis had sent from the house was very different from what they ate. There were stews so delicious he thought it was a pity he could not ask his Chef to taste them.

There were strange sweet-meats of Russian or Persian origin, of which he knew the main ingredients were honey and nuts, and the wine that he had sent was served in goblets which made him stare in astonishment.

"We fashioned these ourselves," the Voivode said as he handed the Marquis a goblet of gold set with semi-precious stones—amethysts, turquoises and cornelians.

There were others ornamented with pink quartz and rock crystal which could be found in the mountains of Russia and the Balkan countries.

"Is it safe to travel with such valuable objects?" the Marquis asked.

The Voivode laughed.

"It would be a brave man who would attack the Gypsies, unless he had a number of soldiers with him!"

The Marquis, glancing at their jewelled-hilted knives, thought that in fact there was good reason for the Gypsies being left severely alone except by the Civil Authorities, backed by the Military.

They ate and drank and, while the men talked

amongst themselves, the women said very little and the Marquis realised that Saviya too was silent.

He took her hand in his and raised it to his lips.

He felt her quiver but still she said nothing, and it was in fact difficult to talk because the Gypsies were singing.

Their voices, melodious and compelling, seemed to raise the tempo so that there was a vibration and excitement in the air.

It grew dark, the stars came out overhead and the moon was creeping up the sky.

The light from the flames of the bonfire, the music vibrating between the trees, the strange clear-cut features and high cheek-bones of those who sang, made a picture that the Marquis thought he would never forget.

Finally the women began to dance.

They were not as graceful or as ethereal as Saviya, but still they were amazingly proficient by any standard.

The Marquis realised that their dances were mostly Russian. Sometimes they were slow, sensuous and as lovely as swans moving over the smooth silvery water of a lake.

At other times they were wildly exhilarating, so that once again he found his heart beating quicker and a strange excitement making him feel as though he danced with them himself.

The music grew wilder, the voices louder, the violins seemed to be a part of the night itself. Then the Voivode rose to his feet.

"You go now," he said to the Marquis.

Saviya put out her arms towards him.

"Shall I ever see you again?" the Marquis heard her whisper.

"It is unlikely," the Voivode answered in English, "but you will be in my thoughts and in my heart, as you have always been."

He held Saviya close to him for one moment. Then

he released her, taking her arms from round his neck and gave her hand to the Marquis.

"She is yours," he said. "Keep her safe."

"I will do that," the Marquis said.

The two men shook hands. Saviya led the Marquis to her caravan.

There were two white horses to draw it, and he climbed up and sat beside her on the front seat. But there were no reins: the horses were led by the Gypsies.

The men playing the violins went ahead and they were followed by the women carrying what looked to the Marquis like bundles and baskets.

The caravan followed and, just as they turned out of sight amongst the trees, the Marquis looked back to see the Voivode standing alone by the fire in the deserted camp.

He leant on his staff and looked very distinguished and at the same time lonely—a King of a very small community, but nevertheless—a King!

The procession wended its way through the trees where it was too dark for the Marquis to see the way. Then finally they came to a stand-still.

The horses were taken from the shafts and, still sitting in the front of the caravan, the Marquis and Saviya watched the women light a small fire.

Those who were carrying the bundles laid them down on the ground beneath the leafy branches of a tree, just out of reach of the heat from the flames.

They laid rugs over the bundles and scattered the flower petals which filled their baskets. They were in every hue of red, pink, white, orange, yellow, and mauve.

Then the Gypsy women danced around the fire, at first slowly and then their movements growing wilder, and more ecstatic.

In the light of the flames their figures had a strange primitive beauty until, to the music of the violins, they moved away into the wood.

The musicians went last and then they too vanished into the darkness of trees.

Saviya stepped down from the caravan to stand beside the fire staring after them.

The Marquis joined her.

The last notes of the violins seemed to hover on the air and then there was silence.

"Did you notice," Saviya asked, her voice very low and lost, "they did not . . . look at me? They will no longer . . . speak to me."

There was so much unhappiness in her voice that the Marquis put his arms around her.

She no longer wore the crown of jewels in which she had been married, and her hair was against his shoulder. He put his hand up very gently to stroke it.

"I am . . . nobody!" she murmured, "I am not even a . . . witch!"

"You are my wife," the Marquis said in a deep voice, "and you have bewitched me, Saviya, from the first moment I saw you. I am caught in your spell and now I can never escape."

He heard her give a deep sigh. She raised her face to his and her eyes were very dark and mysterious in the light of the moon.

"Are you quite sure that it is . . . enough?" she asked. "I have so little to give you. I do not even now know myself."

"But I know you," the Marquis answered. "I know that you are everything I wanted in a woman; everything I desire in my wife. Everything I shall love, adore and worship for the rest of my life."

His words made her quiver and very gently, just as the music had started, soft as the ripple of a raindrop on a smooth pool, he kissed her, holding her against his heart.

Then as he felt a sudden flame rise within her to echo the flame in himself, his lips grew fierce and more demanding.

Wildly, with an elation that was indescribable, he

was kissing her until it was impossible to think of anything save that they were one with each other.

Then as the moon rose higher over the trees and the embers of the fire were red, they lay together on the flower-petalled couch and there was only the whisper of their love.

Chapter Eight

The Marquis rose very quietly so as not to awaken Saviya.

Asleep she looked very young, and he saw the expression on her face was one of intense happiness.

He looked down at her and thought that no-one could be more breathtakingly lovely.

Her eyes were dark half-crescents against the ivory of her skin and her black hair with its blue lights fell over the pillow and her naked shoulders.

They had moved into the caravan just before dawn. A slight breeze had broken the warmth of the night and rustled in the leaves of the trees.

It had been a night of enchantment such as the Marquis had never believed possible.

There was magic in the moonlight, making Saviya look very ethereal, yet also a siren, a Lorelei.

And as their desire for each other swept them away into the heights of ecstasy where there were only the peaks of passion, they were no longer humans, but as gods.

The Marquis put on the long robe which Hobley had brought him when he had been ill in the caravan, and walking through the open door he descended the steps.

The sun illuminated the small clearing and he realised that it was a part of the wood that he had not visited since he was a boy.

Just beyond where the caravan was resting there

was a forest pool surrounded by trees. There were willows overhanging the still water, their leaves almost gold against the dark fir and the silver birch.

Kingcups and wild iris were brilliant yellow on the edge of the pool, and the mosses and lichen beneath the trees were saffron and jade.

It was as lovely in the sunlight as it had been mysterious and unearthly beneath the moon.

Now the Marquis saw that Hobley had already re-lit the fire which had died away during the night, and it was burning brightly, while beyond it was the flower-strewn couch which the Gypsies had made for them.

On it, thrown negligently among the petals, were the jewelled necklaces he had taken from Saviya's neck.

He had loosed her hair, to kiss the scented silk of it and she quivered at the touch of his hands on her body.

'Had there ever been such happiness?' the Marquis asked himself now.

"Good-morning, Hobley," he said aloud.

"Good-morning, M'Lord."

"Did you have much trouble in finding us?" the Marquis asked with a smile.

"It took me some time, M'Lord, but I've brought to Your Lordship the wine for luncheon, it is cooling in the pool."

"Is the water cold?" the Marquis asked.

"Just fresh, M'Lord."

"Then I think I will try it."

He walked towards the pool as he spoke and pulling off his robe, plunged in, finding the water, as Hobley had said, fresh and invigorating and not too chill.

When the Marquis had finished swimming Hobley shaved him, and when finally the valet was no longer required, he went back to the House.

The Marquis sat for a little while staring into the

flames of the fire and then he rose and went to go into
the caravan.

He sat down on the edge of the low bed looking at
Saviya who was still asleep. But after a moment she
opened her eyes.

There was no mistaking the radiance that lit up her
face and as the Marquis bent towards her she made
an inarticulate murmur and put her arms round his
neck.

"It is . . . true!" she whispered. "I was afraid last
night must be only a . . . wonderful dream!"

"Was it wonderful for you, my darling?"

"It was such unbelievable happiness, I did not
know that even love could be so completely perfect."

His lips found hers. Then as he felt her soft and
yielding beneath him, his kiss grew more passionate
and more demanding until everything was forgotten
except their need of each other . . .

It was a long time later that Saviya hurried down
the steps of the caravan towards the fire.

"You must be hungry," she said. "Only the worst
type of wife would allow her husband to be so long
without food."

"I was hungry for something less material!" the Marquis answered and he smiled as Saviya blushed.

She busied herself breaking the eggs Hobley had
brought them and cooked them skilfully over the fire.

But all the time she was aware that the Marquis
was watching her, and she was conscious that she
wore only a silk wrap and her hair was falling loose
on either side of her small face.

"You make me shy," she protested.

"I adore you when you are shy."

She waited on him and he ate all she gave him.
Then as she laid aside the plates and the cooking pans
he said:

"Leave those for Hobley, Saviya. I want you."

She smiled at him provokingly.

"Are you commanding me?"

"Of course! Are you defying me?"

"What would you do if I did?"

"Carry you away into the dungeons of my Castle and torture you until you surrendered yourself completely and unreservedly. I love you to distraction, my lovely, but I will be your master."

She looked at him uncertainly, not quite sure if he was joking or serious.

"Come here, my precious," he said softly.

And then she ran into his arms like a child seeking safety.

As the hours passed they lay in the sun-shine talking of themselves and their love.

Late in the day when it grew hotter, the Marquis persuaded Saviya to swim in the pool.

As she moved across it he thought that nothing could be more lovely than the perfection of her white body beneath the silver ripples.

It made her seem part of the trees, the irises and the darkness of the woods. When finally she came from the pool, the water glistening on her body like dew-drops, he held her close as if he was afraid of losing her.

"I am convinced now," he said in his deep voice, "that you are a wood-nymph and if I do not hold on you will vanish like the morning mist, and I shall never be able to find you again."

She pressed herself against him, her arms round his neck and he kissed her at first gently, then fiercely, demandingly, until finally he picked her up in his arms to carry her back to the flower-strewn couch on which they had spent the night.

It was late in the afternoon when the Marquis said:

"We must go now, my darling."

"Go? Go where?"

"Home," he replied. "We are to be married."

"We are married!"

"We are, I agree, joined together irrevocably," the Marquis answered. "But at the same time I wish to marry you, Saviya, according to the Law of England, and receive the blessing of the Church—my Church, which I hope one day will also be yours."

She was silent for a moment, her head bent a little as if she searched for words. Then she said:

"As you know, the ceremony yesterday when we intermingled our blood is to me sacred and unites us in a manner which means that I belong to you and could never belong to anyone else. But for you it is different?"

"There is no difference," the Marquis said firmly.

"But there is," she answered. "You do not acknowledge the Gypsy laws which for me are binding, even though I am no longer a Gypsy. And because of your position in the world, because you are of such importance, it is best that you could, if you wished it, be free to marry a woman of your own class."

"You are my class! We are both equally well bred," the Marquis said. "I always believed it even before the Voivode told us his tale."

He lifted her chin with his fingers until she was looking up at him.

"Have you forgotten," he asked, "that when you were exchanged for the dead baby, the Voivode said that you were the child of a nobleman?"

"I am still nameless—still nobody!" Saviya replied miserably. "Let me stay with you because I am yours, but it is best if I do not become your wife according to English Law, so that your friends must acknowledge my position even while they despise me for myself."

"No-one will despise you as far as I am concerned," the Marquis said with a hard note in his voice.

"I can never forget," Saviya said, "the way your cousin referred to me. He was only speaking aloud what your friends and acquaintances will have been thinking even though they are too tactful or too frightened to say it to your face."

"I have told you before, and I must say it again," the Marquis said, "that I am not in the least interested

171

what anyone should say behind my back. I honour and respect you. You are, in every way, all I have ever wished my wife to be."

He saw the troubled expression in Saviya's eyes and added:

"I am not prepared to argue about this, Saviya. You obeyed the Voivode and you will obey me. You are mine and it is for me to make the decisions which affect our lives."

Her eyes were on his and he felt that she was glad that he was so masterful, and that she must obey his authority as she had obeyed the Chief of her tribe.

"I will do . . . anything you ask of me," she said softly after a moment.

And because she was so pliant and so sweet, the Marquis crushed her against him and kissed her until the world whirled around them and once again everything was forgotten but themselves.

When they were dressed they walked a little way through the wood and found on the bridle-path the Marquis's Phaeton.

He helped Saviya into it, took the reins from the groom who jumped up behind. They moved forward.

The Marquis could only drive slowly until they were clear of the trees, but when they reached the Park he tooled his horses swiftly with an expertise that made Saviya look at him appreciatively.

He knew she was delighted with the horse-flesh he kept in his stables, and he planned that as soon as they returned from their honeymoon he would buy her some horses for her own. He knew exactly the type of Arab-bred animal which would suit her.

Ruckley House looked exquisite in the late afternoon sunshine.

Already the shadows were growing longer on the green lawns and the flowers were great patches of colour. The house itself glowed warm and welcoming as a jewel.

The flag was flying on the roof-tops and Saviya looked up at it with a little smile.

"Your flag!" she said, remembering how angry he had been when Jethro had flown it in his absence.

"Our flag!" he corrected, "over our house, my darling."

"Can I really own a part of anything so beautiful?" Saviya asked.

"Everything I have is yours," the Marquis replied.

"I think I have always longed for a house of my own," Saviya told him. "Perhaps it was some forgotten instinct or a part of my blood, but for me home has always meant a place where I could stay and not have to move on."

She gave a little laugh that was half a sigh.

"Perhaps really I have never been a Gypsy at heart. I only thought I was. I am beginning to understand now so many things about myself which puzzled me."

"I want to know everything you feel and everything you think," the Marquis said. "I cannot bear that any part of you should not be mine."

"It is all . . . yours," Saviya whispered.

The Marquis drew up at the front door with a flourish.

As they both alighted from the Phaeton he held out his hand to Saviya and they walked up the steps hand in hand.

She was wearing the elaborate, exquisitely embroidered Gypsy dress in which she had been married, and the Marquis had fastened the jewelled necklaces around her neck and the jewelled ear-rings in her small ears.

Only her head was bare, because the crown in which she had married was part of the Kalderash treasure and was used for every wedding which took place within the tribe.

"There are three gentlemen waiting for Your Lordship," Bush said, as they reached the Hall. "They are in the Salon."

"Visitors?" the Marquis asked sharply.

"Captain Collington brought them, M'Lord. They arrived just after luncheon and I told them that

Your Lordship was expected later in the afternoon."

The Marquis smiled.

"Charles is here!" he said to Saviya. "I wrote to him yesterday to tell him I was alive. I felt that he would be unable to resist coming to make sure for himself."

Still holding Saviya's hand the Marquis walked towards the Salon, and as the door was opened for them by a footman, they entered.

There were three men at the far end of the room and as the Marquis and Saviya entered they sprang to their feet.

"Fabius, I have never been so glad of anything in my whole life, as I was to get your note!" Charles Collington exclaimed.

He hurried across the room to the Marquis as he spoke, both hands outstretched.

"You are all right?" he added, the Marquis's hand in his.

"I have completely recovered, thanks to Saviya," the Marquis answered, "but it was a near thing."

"His Lordship told me how wonderful you have been," Charles Collington said to Saviya.

She smiled at him as he lifted her hand to his lips.

"I and all of Fabius's friends owe you a great debt of gratitude," he said with great sincerity.

While he was speaking, the Marquis went towards the two other gentlemen standing in front of the fireplace.

One of them was Sir Algernon Gibbon—the other, the Marquis realised, was a man he had never seen before.

"I have heard the amazing story of your preservation from death!" Sir Algernon said. "When your cousin told me you had been ambushed in the wood and murdered by Saviya I could not credit it was the truth, but there was nothing I could do to refute his assertion."

"All is well that ends well," the Marquis said

briefly, as if he had no wish to go on discussing what had happened in the past.

He looked enquiringly at the stranger standing beside Sir Algernon.

"I want to introduce," Sir Algernon said pompously, "the Earl of Glencairn whom I have brought here for a very special reason."

The Marquis held out his hand, but to his surprise the man who had just been introduced was not looking at him but at Saviya who was approaching them across the room talking animatedly to Charles Collington.

He was staring at her in such a strange manner that the Marquis's hand fell to his side.

Then, as if everyone realised that something strange and untoward was happening, there was silence until the Earl of Glencairn exclaimed in a voice that was somehow constricted:

"It is incredible!"

Then to Saviya he said:

"You are exactly like your mother!"

Saviya stared at him wide-eyed until Sir Algernon, feeling that the onus for explanation was on him, said:

"Saviya, the Earl of Glencairn wishes to see your birth-mark—the head of the hawk that you showed me when I was here before."

"There is no reason for her to show it," the Earl of Glencairn said before Saviya could reply. "This is my daughter, who I thought was dead but about whom I only learnt the truth six years ago when my second wife died."

"I . . . I am . . . your daughter?" Saviya asked in a voice that was hardly above a whisper.

"You are my daughter," the Earl of Glencairn said firmly.

"Then . . . I have a . . . name?"

"You have indeed," he answered. "You are the Lady Conchita McCairn, and my eldest child who I believed had died when she was fifteen months old.

When I learnt you had been given to the Gypsies I believed that you were lost to me forever."

Saviya was very pale and, almost as if she was afraid of what was being revealed, she put her hand on the Marquis's arm.

He covered her fingers reassuringly with his own and said:

"As you are Saviya's father, My Lord, I think it right that you should know we have already been united by a Gypsy marriage. Now I would ask your permission for her to be my wife according to the laws of this country."

"Must I lose my daughter having only just found her?" the Earl asked, but he smiled as he spoke.

"How did you find me?" Saviya asked.

"You can thank me for that," Sir Algernon Gibbon said proudly. "When the Marquis and Charles Collington thought they had won a thousand pounds from me because they had passed off a Gypsy as a Lady of Quality, I was prepared to acknowledge myself the loser and pay my debt."

"You were indeed very sporting about it," Charles Collington said irrepressibly.

"I am glad you thought so," Sir Algernon Gibbon replied, "but I was also quite certain that my contention was right, and that Saviya was in fact the possessor of blue blood."

"How could you have thought that?" the Marquis said.

"Because," Sir Algernon answered, "I knew in the back of my mind, when it was first mentioned, there was one family somewhere in the Kingdom whose members carried somewhere on their person the mark of the hawk."

"I thought it . . . showed that I was a . . . witch!" Saviya murmured.

"On the contrary," Sir Algernon said, "after some thought I remembered that it showed that you were a McCairn."

"It is quite true," the Earl interposed. "The birth-mark occurs all down the ages, not on every member of the Clan, of course, and more often amongst the females than the males. In any case it happens and our crest is the hawk's head."

"We must be very grateful," the Marquis interposed, "for your amazing knowledge of genealogy, Gibbon."

"When I remembered the history of the McCairn birth-mark," Sir Algernon said, "I wrote to the Earl asking to see him. He replied that he was coming to London and would call on me. By the time I received his letter your death was being proclaimed by your cousin, Jethro, and there was a warrant out for Saviya's arrest."

"I should still have wanted to find her," the Earl said.

"Fortunately, I did not have to upset you with such a disturbing story," Sir Algernon replied, "because while I was wondering what excuse I should make for dragging you to London, Charles Collington heard yesterday from the Marquis and I was able to give you good news of your daughter instead of bad."

"It is very good news indeed," the Earl exclaimed and to Saviya he said:

"If you only knew how much I have suffered these past six years!"

"Had you no idea that the baby which was buried was not your own?" the Marquis asked.

"None at all!" the Earl answered. "Actually I was away from home at the time and only returned the very day of the funeral which had been arranged by my wife, Conchita's step-mother."

"And I imagine the old nurse told you exactly what happened," the Marquis said. "We have heard the story from the Voivode, the Chief of the Kalderash, who brought Saviya up as his own child."

"I want to hear every detail," Charles Collington cried. "When did you and Saviya learn that she was in fact not a Gypsy as she had thought herself to be? There is a lot of explaining to do."

"There is indeed," the Marquis answered, "but there is one thing I want to ask before we go any further and I think it is a question uppermost in all our minds."

"What is that?" the Earl enquired.

"Why is Saviya so dark?" the Marquis enquired. "She does not resemble you in the least."

"No indeed," the Earl answered.

His hair was almost white but it was obvious that when he was young it would have been the pale red that was essentially Scottish.

He also possessed blue eyes and a fair complexion. Sturdily built with square shoulders, it seemed almost impossible for the slim, small-boned Saviya with her jet-black hair to be his child.

"The explanation is very simple," he said. "My wife was Spanish."

"Spanish!" Sir Algernon ejaculated, "why did I not think of that?"

"It did not occur to any of us," the Marquis admitted.

"My family has always owned land in Spain," the Earl went on. "It is near Segovia. When I visited it as a young man I fell in love with a most entrancing Contessa. I brought her back to Scotland but she died when our child was born."

He paused and said to Saviya in a voice deep with emotion:

"When I saw you walk across the room just now you might in fact have been your mother. The resemblance is almost uncanny."

"Now tell us the whole story," Charles Collington insisted. "From the very beginning."

The Marquis related briefly what the Voivode had revealed to him and Saviya only the day before.

"It was Conchita's old nurse who told me the truth six years ago after my second wife died," the Earl said on the completion of the Marquis's story. "What you have just related exactly bears out her tale."

He smiled at Saviya who had been listening wide-eyed.

178

"There is only one thing I have to add," he went on, "which I hope, my dear, will not disappoint you. It is that you are not my heir."

"Why not, now that you have found her again?" Charles Collington asked impulsively.

"Because," the Earl replied, "I have married for the third time and two years ago my wife, who is a good deal younger than I am, presented me with twin sons. There is therefore a male McCairn to inherit the Earldom."

"I am glad," the Marquis said. "I do not wish my wife to be concerned with any Estate save my own!"

As he spoke he looked at the clock on the mantelshelf and rose to his feet.

"The Reverend will be ready for us in my private Chapel in exactly half an hour's time. I feel, My Lord, that you would wish to give your daughter away, and what could be more appropriate than that my best man should be my oldest friend?"

He smiled at Charles and went on:

"And that the witness to the ceremony should be Sir Algernon Gibbon, whose exceptional knowledge of ancient family characteristics has brought my future wife and her father together?"

The Marquis took Saviya by the arm and drew her towards the door.

"Upstairs, my darling," he said quietly, "you will find a white gown which I ordered from London yesterday, along with some other clothes which I hope will please you. They come from the same dress-maker who provided the green dress in which we attempted and failed to deceive Sir Algernon."

"I can hardly believe that all this is true!" Saviya told him. "Now I am no longer ashamed to be your wife."

"There was never anything of which you need have been ashamed," the Marquis replied, "but if the knowledge that you are of noble Scottish descent makes you happy, then it makes me happy, too."

He lifted her hands to his lips and kissed her fingers one by one.

She looked into his eyes and for a moment they were both very still.

"I love you!" the Marquis said below his breath, "and I want to be alone with you."

"I want it . . . too!" Saviya whispered.

Then with an effort she drew her hands from his and went up the stairs.

It was nearly mid-night when the Marquis dismissed Hobley.

There had been so much to talk about after the wedding; so much to hear both from Saviya and her father that the hours had sped by.

Their wedding had been very beautiful.

The Chapel at Ruckley House had been built at the same time as the house itself, and the carved pews and beautiful reredos behind the Altar had remained unchanged down the centuries.

There had been the soft music of an organ, very unlike the throbbing melody of the violins, viola and sitar which had been part of the ceremony of the night before.

But there had been an atmosphere of faith and devotion in the small Chapel. The candles glowing brightly illuminated Saviya's lovely face covered by a lace veil that had been in the Ruckley family for centuries.

There had been a tiara of diamonds on her dark hair, diamonds to encircle her neck and glitter in her ears, and her bouquet had been of white lilies.

She had looked beautiful but also so conventional that it was hard to remember they had ever imagined her to be a wild, uncivilised Gypsy.

The Marquis had repeated his vows in a firm, strong voice that seemed to echo round the Chapel.

Saviya's tone had been soft but at the same time there had been such a deep sincerity in the way she spoke which brought, the Marquis thought, a new solemnity to their relationship.

On The Reverend's advice and to please the Earl,

Saviya used her real name which had been given her at her Christening and which had also been her mother's.

But because the Marquis would never be able to think of her except as Saviya, she said:

"I, Conchita Saviya, take thee, Fabius Alexander, to be my wedded husband . . ."

Last night the Marquis had not given her a ring, but tonight, his mother's ring was on the third finger of her left hand, and he felt that it bound them even closer to each other than they had been before.

'You are mine, mine by every law and vow that could unite us with each other,' the Marquis wanted to cry.

Instead, when the ceremony had ended, he lifted Saviya's veil and kissed her very gently on the lips.

He knew then that she was as moved as he was.

It had seemed that there was a new dignity and authority in The Reverend that neither of them had known before, and by the sanctity of his office they were now husband and wife, in the real sense of the word, and no-one could ever put them asunder.

"I love you!" the Marquis whispered as, with Saviya on his arm, they walked from the Chapel and down the corridor which led to the more familiar part of the house.

"I am your wife!" she said, "and now I want everyone to know that I am yours and that I am who I am!"

"It shall be in *The Gazette* the day after tomorrow," the Marquis said with a smile, "and then there will be no doubt in anyone's mind as to whom I have married."

"You know I am not thinking of myself," she whispered, "but of you."

"I know that," he answered, "but I am glad for your sake, my beloved, as well as for mine. Now you have a background. Now you have roots. Now you have a whole family and a Clan!"

"You are trying to frighten me!" she said accusing-

181

ly, but her eyes were shining.

"I am only reminding you that you have taken on many heavy responsibilities," the Marquis said. "There will be no more wandering carefree over the world!"

"If you talk like that I shall run away from you!" she threatened, but he knew she was only teasing.

"You will never leave me," he answered seriously, "because you know I could not live without you. You will be with me always, Saviya, and because we have so nearly lost each other, I will never let you out of my sight."

She laughed a little at that, but she knew that it was true.

She had not only nearly lost him through the murderous intentions of his cousin, but also, believing it was in his best interests, she had attempted to run away with her tribe and break the bond which bound them to each other by some indefinable magic.

After the wedding they had dinner, but it was a very different feast from the one they had enjoyed the night before.

Course succeeded course, served by powdered footmen on crested, silver dishes. There had been champagne to drink, but now it was in crystal glasses and not in the fabulous jewelled goblets from which they had drunk around the fire in the woods.

The Earl of Glencairn told them stories of the McCairn Clan; their fights and feuds and the part they had played in Scottish history.

Sir Algernon related strange signs which other families besides the McCairns bore, and repeated again and again how delighted he was that it was his knowledge which had united Saviya and her father.

There was so much to talk about; so much that was interesting and amusing. But the Marquis did not only wish to be alone with Saviya; he also remembered that the following day they were starting on a journey that would carry them to Spain.

"It is strange that I should have chosen Spain for our honeymoon," he said to the Earl.

"You must visit Conchita's relations," the Earl replied. "I will give you letters of introduction and you will learn if you have not visited Spain before how very beautiful its women are."

"To be aware of that I have only to look at my wife," the Marquis answered.

It had been altogether a very satisfactory day, he told himself, when finally he knocked gently on the communicating door between his own and Saviya's bed-rooms and without waiting for an answer entered.

The room was in darkness save for the light from the flames in the fireplace.

It might have been expected, the Marquis thought, that Saviya would have a fire. It was so much a part of the Gypsy way of life, it was in fact almost a sacred symbol amongst them.

But the heat of the day had passed and tonight there was a chill wind blowing outside, so the fire was in fact a necessity.

He walked across the room and in the darkness the bedposts reminded him of the trunks of the trees which had encircled them last night.

Saviya was sitting on a white bear-skin rug in front of the fire.

The Marquis noticed that she had pulled the cushions from the chairs and placed them around her.

But she was sitting upright, her long dark hair covering her to below the waist.

There was the scent of flowers but now they were in vases on the side-tables. There was also the exotic fragrance of Saviya's hair, that strange, haunting perfume which the Marquis had noticed that first time when he carried her in his arms after he had knocked her down with his Phaeton.

He stood looking down at her, very tall and handsome in his long brocade robe.

As she lifted her face there was a smile on her lips and an expression in her eyes which made his heart turn over in his breast.

"You are very beautiful, my precious."

There was a depth in his voice to which she vibrated.

"I want you to . . . think so."

"Could I ever think anything else?"

The firelight was on her face and he wondered if any other woman could look so alluring, so mysterious and at the same time so utterly and completely desirable.

There was a sudden gust of wind in the chimney and the creeper outside the windows tapped against one of the panes.

"There is a cold wind tonight," the Marquis said in an absent-minded voice as if he was thinking of something else. "I am glad we will sleep in a bed."

"Are you sure of . . . that?" Saviya asked.

Now he saw there was that faintly mocking smile on her lips that had entranced him when they had first met.

He reached down to lift her to her feet but as he did so her arms went round his neck and she pulled him down to her.

"Saviya!" he said hoarsely.

Then he felt her lips seek his and as his mouth took possession of her he could feel her heart beating against his.

"I love you!" he wanted to say.

But he was swept away by an indescribable magic —a spell so blinding, so compelling that they were both lost in an ecstasy and rapture for which there were no words.

ABOUT THE AUTHOR

BARBARA CARTLAND, the celebrated romantic author, historian, playwright, lecturer, political speaker and television personality, has now written over 150 books. Miss Cartland has had a number of historical books published and several biographical ones, including that of her brother, Major Ronald Cartland, who was the first Member of Parliament to be killed in the War. This book had a Foreword by Sir Winston Churchill.

In private life, Barbara Cartland, who is a Dame of the Order of St. John of Jerusalem, has fought for better conditions and salaries for Midwives and Nurses. As President of the Royal College of Midwives (Hertfordshire Branch), she has been invested with the first Badge of Office ever given in Great Britain, which was subscribed to by the Midwives themselves. She has also championed the cause for old people and founded the first Romany Gypsy Camp in the world.

Barbara Cartland is deeply interested in Vitamin Therapy and is President of the British National Association for Health.